Please, no zits!

and other short stories for LDS youth

Please, no zits!

and other short stories for LDS youth

by

Anne Bradshaw

Golden Wings Enterprises

This is a work of fiction, and the views expressed herein are the sole responsibility of the author. Likewise, characters, places, and incidents are either the product of the author's imagination or are represented fictitiously, and any resemblance to actual persons, living or dead, or actual events or locales, is entirely coincidental.

Please, no zits!
and other short stories for LDS youth

Published by

GoldenWings

Golden Wings Enterprises
P.O. Box 468, Orem, Utah 84059-0468

Cover design copyright © 2007 by Glade Cox

GoldenWings is a registered trademark of Golden Wings Enterprises

Copyright © 2007 by Anne Bradshaw

ISBN 978-0-9794340-0-6

Printed in the United States of America
Year of first printing: 2007

10 9 8 7 6 5 4 3 2 1

For some of the best people this side of heaven . . .

OUR YOUTH.

Enjoy!

Acknowledgements

How thankful I am for kind friends at LDStorymakers who believed these stories could make a difference in the lives of LDS youth—especially editors Shirley Bahlmann, Lisa J. Peck, Julie Wright, and BJ Rowley. Many thanks also to author Julie Bellon and her family (Jeff, Lauren, and Jared) for help with American English. And a special thanks to Glade, Oliver, Jordan, and Pete for their fun cover images.

There is one story I feel deserves particular mention, found on page 25: *Rock Bottom in a Jail Cell*. Bishop Keith Bassett, a former police officer now living in Devon, England, provided background details for this poignant tale of substance abuse. Sue Rudd from New Oscott, England, offered helpful advice with the British dialect. And author/songwriter Kristine Litster Fales, now living in Boise, Idaho, whose *Wings of Glory: Hope and Healing from Addiction* (music CD & book set) is helping countless youth facing situations similar to those of Alex, provided accurate addiction feedback with the help of her son, Jonathan Fales. More details about Kristine's work can be found at: www.WingsOfGlory.net

I'm grateful to the New Era magazine staff, who for years published my fiction when it was part of their magazine content. They were an answer to prayers when my work began. I thank my Heavenly Father daily for blessings that come from writing and reading.

And, of course, my heartfelt thanks to all the young (and not-so-young) readers who take time to explore these stories. May your lives be filled with the Light you need for a great experience here on earth.

Contents

The stories in this book are set in the United States,
England, Scotland, Ireland, and Wales.
Terminologies used are culturally accurate.
(See page 130 for Word List and page 10 for British Isles map)

Chapter			Page

THE
BRITISH ISLES

Inverness

SCOTLAND

Edinburgh

N.
IRELAND
Belfast

Mucker
Village

Liverpool
Manchester

Dublin

Anglesey

Sutton Coldfield

IRELAND

Birmingham

Clent Hills

WALES

ENGLAND

London

Sussex Downs

Milford-on-Sea

Exeter

Chapter 1

Apple Pie and Chocolate Corners

(Muker Village, Yorkshire, England)

Dad's voice was loud and curt, bloodshot eyes narrowed, flashing danger. "You're not going to that youth conference, Reuben, and that's final." His thin, weather-beaten body straightened to its full height, and his mouth clamped in a hard line.

I bit my lip, digging the heel of my boot into the dirt.

"And if I hear any more about it, you can tell that Rob lad to stop picking you up for church Wednesdays. You're slow enough at school without that . . . that . . . seminary stuff taking your time."

He stomped past the hen sheds, muttering to himself. "Should never have let you join that church in the first place. Not been the same since. Always trying to change things." He tore down a dead branch overhanging the path, swishing it violently. "As if I haven't got enough problems without you pestering about a conference. I'm sick of it, do you hear? *Sick* of it!" He snapped the branch across his knee.

Squawking hens scattered in all directions. One rushed terror-stricken into a pile of loose wire netting. I'd left it there this morning when the school bus arrived before I was ready. Okay, so I was late—same thing. Anyway, I never finished the job properly.

"Now look what you've done," Dad yelled. "Can't you do anything right? That's all we need—a hen with a broken wing." He grabbed the screeching hen and marched back toward the house. "Get on with the chores," he flung over his shoulder, "and keep out of my way."

The twisted, choking feeling in my stomach moved to my throat and stuck there. I hadn't cried since Mum died in a car accident nine years ago, and I wasn't about to begin now. We used to live on a farm in Devon back then, but after the funeral we moved north to Muker Village, Yorkshire. It had been so cold here. Seemed like Dad was forever mad at someone for taking Mum, and I was the one who got it every time things went wrong.

I really thought today was a safe time to ask about the youth conference. I'd never been to one, but imagined my sixteenth birthday was important enough for Dad to agree. No such luck. In fact, the only bright moment was getting that card at break-fast. No one ever bothered to send me one before. Come to think of it, no one ever believed in me at all before this new seminary lady moved into the branch. She seemed to understand that I wasn't as slow as I looked—perhaps because she was an artist, like me.

Dad didn't care for my drawing. "Waste of time," he called it. So I never sketched when he was around, but sometimes he caught me anyway. The other day I had been sure he was down the bottom field fixing fences. I'd noticed a bunch of tiny pansies poking through cracks in the concrete by our goat shed earlier in the week, and waited my chance to draw them in their gentle strength.

That day, I sat near the pansies and drank in the smell of dew-covered grass mixed with fresh hay. Even the whiff of goatskin added something good to the fresh spring air. I was penciling in lines of shape and shadow when Dad's furious roar sent my papers flying.

"Can't leave you alone for ten minutes without you letting me down." His muddy boot slammed into the upturned page. "Now get up. If you've no jobs and your schoolwork's finished, then at least turn your hand to something useful."

I grabbed the ruined work and trudged to my room. My thoughts were not worthy ones. It was all very well learning how to handle these things in church, but when it came to real life . . . First, it was hard remembering the feeling I *should* be having, and then it was even harder making it happen. How was I supposed to feel friendly and loving when someone shot evil words at me? There must be a secret to it, but I wasn't sure I really wanted to find out.

I wasn't even sure I wanted to stay around here any longer. Maybe Dad's brother down in Portsmouth would take me in— though sharing the Church with him would be even more difficult than sharing it with Dad.

By the time Wednesday came, I'd done some thinking. I'd kept out of Dad's way for days, and almost decided to pack my bags the following Friday—Dad's night at the pub. I'd also given in to the idea that I ought to attend seminary one last time, if only to thank Sister Wilson for the card.

I edged my way into the back row. I would miss this crowd— especially Katie, third row from the front. Her smile seemed sweeter for me than for anyone else. Pity I wouldn't get to know her better.

The lesson didn't start out too exciting—all that talk about reaching the highest degree of glory. My mind switched off when those Sunday words began. Other things were on my mind—like working out a different way to milk the goat. It was all this growing that was the problem. My head used to rest comfy on the bulge of the goat's stomach, and I milked with my eyes shut, dreaming. But now, my head poked above her bony back, and my chin didn't rest easy on that ridged spine of hers.

Sister Wilson was going on a bit. Her long black hair swung, glinting in the sunlight as she moved. I leaned back, half following the words and enjoying the expressions crisscrossing her face.

Then, all of a sudden, she produced this piece of pie, oozing bubbly juice, and thick with chunky apple piled between covers of crumbling pastry. *And* there was a dollop of cream on top.

Whatever was she planning to do with that? I sniffed the

sweet cinnamon smell. There wasn't enough for us all. I glanced at the others. All eyes opened wide. They were definitely paying attention.

"I'm about to give this to one student," Sister Wilson said. "Let me see now . . . Reuben? Looks like all that farm work is stretching you fast. I'm sure your stomach could manage this pie"

Had I lucked out or what? I was sure she'd give it to Rob. He was the smart lad, the one whose hand flew up at every question and who knew every scripture the week before we were asked to learn it. It was his mum who sent the Elders our way a couple of years ago.

If not him, then surely Sarah? Sarah did everything right. Her work was always handed in on time.

But me? I didn't need asking twice. That pie disappeared faster than corn in a henhouse. And I felt twenty-two eyes watching every mouthful. I sat back, rubbing my stomach. She was right—it had stretched lately.

Then she asked a weird question. "How do the rest of you feel at this moment?"

I mean, how did she expect them to feel? Sick, I should think. Like they'd been cheated out of something amazing. At least, that's what Rob said, and the others nodded. They weren't too cheerful.

"Good," Sister Wilson said. "Remember that feeling every time you're tempted by the Adversary, because it's one you might get, only worse, if you don't make it past the terrestrial kingdom when you die."

That pulled me up short, made prickles creep up and down my spine. The feelings I'd enjoyed munching that pie were great. Maybe there was something to all this.

* * *

I never did leave home. Weeks went by, and the apple pie memory faded, slipping into a corner somewhere in my mind—a bit like my drawing collection. The best ones got pulled out and stared at now and again, but stayed shut in the cupboard most of the time.

If it weren't for the accident, the apple pie corner would have stayed hidden a lot longer.

It was a Saturday morning. I remember, because Dad got drunk at the pub the night before. I was down the yard at five thirty milking Mrs. Nephi. I named her that because Nephi found wild goats in the Promised Land. I often wondered whether he liked them as much as I did. He cared for outsiders, and no one else in the scriptures ever thought much of goats.

I'd found a good spot to rest my chin—there was an extra lump of gristle to one side of Mrs. Nephi's backbone that's softer than the rest—when suddenly this fox appeared, rushing in front of us.

Well. Old Mrs. Nephi went wild, staggering sideways, and then stumbling across the wooden stand. I hadn't bothered tethering her. She never moved an inch normally, but gazed into the distance, grinding her teeth round and round like some old lady enjoying her memory.

This time, back legs bucked, hooves clattered down into the bucket, and milk sloshed all over. My head snapped back, and I fell off the stool, crashing into the heavy gate beam that stood wedged against the goat shed.

The beam toppled, missed my neck by inches, but hit my arm, crushing the bone with wicked pain. I remember screaming in agony until things went swimmy and black.

My shrieks must have been right powerful. Only something dreadful could waken Dad on a Saturday morning. Next thing I knew he was leaning close, yelling my name.

Somehow he got me to the hospital, ten miles away. I never, ever, want to drive in that condition again. The pain was terrible, bumping over those country roads. I wanted to whimper like a child. Only the sight of Dad's tight-lipped face forced back my cries.

Sister Wilson could have used an experience like mine when we did that scripture on suffering, in the Doctrine and Covenants nineteen something-or-other. And to think my agony was nothing compared to the Saviour's. I dared not imagine His pain—and all for the likes of me and my dad. So I pulled out those apple pie thoughts to check them through again. I didn't want to miss knowing someone who loved me that much.

The day after my accident, Dad opened the front door to find Sister Wilson on the doorstep. I heard her from my makeshift bed on the sofa.

"Why, hello, Mr. Bell." She didn't give him a chance to slam the door but kept right on talking. "I've brought this pie to cheer up Reuben. I know he's fond of apples. Can you help him eat it?"

If there was one thing Dad and I had in common, it was appreciation for apple pies.

"I . . . um . . . that's right good of you, Miss . . . uh . . ."

"The name's Jenny, Mr. Bell. I'm Reuben's seminary teacher, I—"

"Very kind of you, yes, most kind." Dad's tongue loosened fast. "But I'm sorry, you can't see the lad. He's—"

"Sister Wilson!" I called out, guessing the lie he was about to offer. "Hello! Thanks for coming. Is that for us? Can you stop a minute? How's Katie? How's the class? How's . . . ?"

I ran out of questions, but Dad was opening the door again, stepping aside with a sheepish look on his face.

She came again and again. Each time Dad softened more. I didn't know Sister Wilson cared for animals so much. She even knew how to milk Mrs. Nephi.

Good job she got on the right side of Dad though, because he wouldn't have let the home teachers round for anyone else but her. And that blessing they gave me. I don't remember getting a feeling like that before. The warmth rushed clear through to my toenails.

Now, I'd heard Sister Wilson mention miracles, but I never thought I'd ever get one. And I healed all right—so fast the doctors weren't sure what went on. They were sure that such a messy break would never mend straight.

But it did.

Dad was equally amazed. And as incredible as it may seem, he even looked at my seminary booklets one day while I worked on them. I wanted to keep doing them, despite the arm. I couldn't let Sister Wilson down, not after she'd gone to so much trouble. Besides, she always made me feel kind of important. I enjoyed that. Belonging somehow.

I promised myself something as soon as my arm was strong and I was milking Mrs. Nephi again. Somehow, I would learn those Scripture Mastery verses. With each squeeze and squirt, I repeated a scripture reference until they were all set in my brain.

Today, our class finished for the year. I gave Sister Wilson a box of chocolates. She looked sort of choked, and I heard her sniff. I turned away to hide my red cheeks. On thinking it over, perhaps it was the words, not the chocolates, that made her cry.

"Sister Wilson," I said, "I've decided to start saving for a mission. I want to take part in *all* the blessings of eternity. Not only that, but I want to help others feel they're important to someone. You know what I mean?"

She nodded, her lips quivering, then dabbed her eyes with the back of her hand.

"Oh, and by the way . . ." I finished in a rush because my own eyes weren't too dry, either, "Dad says, if I earn half, he . . . he'll pay the rest."

I left the room faster than normal, but not before I glimpsed her face. It glowed with such a strange look. Was that the joy she was always on about?

Maybe her mind had a corner for chocolate. I liked the idea of being a memory that's pulled out now and again.

Chapter 2

Better Fish in the Sea

(Milford-on-Sea, Hampshire, England)

The sad cry of seagulls disturbed my thoughts as I lay, warmly dressed in jeans and thick red sweater, on the beach at Milford-on-Sea. I'd found a sheltered place by a sea break and was glad of time to be alone with my problem.

A flock of wheeling gulls blocked the sun. I brushed my hand across closed eyes, trying to wipe away the sight of them, wishing the same could be done with last night's memories.

James, with his gold rings and expensive suit, was not his usual, charming self. "Standards!" he shouted, as we said goodnight in the car. "I'm sick of them. Either you love me or you don't. We can live together same as other people outside your church. No more playing around. I want the answer tomorrow."

There was barely time to close the door before he accelerated away.

I stood and walked along the seashore. The wind smelled of damp seaweed. I rubbed sea spray from my cheeks, determined not to cry. All my life I'd heard about this kind of thing, but never thought it would happen to me.

I replayed an old argument with my mum over and over in my head.

"Please, Mum, I'm seventeen. Can't I make up my own mind? Everyone else in my school class will be at the party."

Mum's forehead creased. "It's not that I don't trust you, Susie. I know you have high standards. It's simply—"

"I know, I know," I said, rolling my eyes. *" The atmosphere's all wrong. But they accept that I don't drink, and there's nothing going on at church in our ward. I mean, Kent and Graham are fine, but not to date. Actually, James said we're going."* I looked down.

"Susie, there will *be opportunities to meet LDS youth around the country. And there's an old saying—'you marry your date, so date someone you might marry.' Remember?"*

"Oh, come on! Marriage? I want a good time—you know—a boy friend. Why can't you understand?"

Mother shrugged and pressed her lips tight.

I moved closer to the water's edge, watching seagulls dodge swishing waves. Wormholes kept popping up, bursting with bubbles. The birds poked with their dangerous beaks, grabbing at the creatures, sucking them out. I whispered to the worms, "I know how you feel."

Hadn't James done the same to me?

"I don't like your church friends, Susie," he said. *"They need to lighten up."*

My face went hot.

He went on. "They need to grow up. There's a whole world out there. A different kind of fun waiting for you and me."

I bent to remove my trainers, then trailed along the beach, bare feet pushing against rippling ridges left by waves. What was it Dad used to say when I was small? Copy the crabs. Walk sideways, and your feet won't feel the bumps.

It was like that at home for a while—walking sideways to avoid bumping my feelings for James against Mum and Dad. But eventually they collided.

"Susie, Susie," James had murmured against my hair as we embraced on the doorstep a few weeks ago. A kiss was beginning when the door opened.

Dad stood there in his pyjamas. "Ah, Susie, you're home. I was getting uneasy, my dear."

James jumped back. "Sorry, Mr. Blake. We meant to be here by eleven thirty, but the traffic was bad," he lied. *He pushed me forward, laughing. "See you tomorrow, Sue. Pick you up at seven. My mate's getting a video. We're invited to his place."*

*He jumped down all three steps at once, stopping at the bottom,
swinging around. "Don't worry, Mr. Blake, I'll have her home by
eleven thirty next time." He grinned, dived into his silver mini,
revved the engine, hit the horn, and was gone.*

*I tried to move upstairs with the same kind of speed, but Dad's
voice stopped me.*

*"One moment, young lady." He locked the front door. "Come in
the lounge a minute. I'd like a few words."*

*We sat on the sofa. "It's not what you think," I began. "James
would never hurt me. He's only a friend. We're—"*

*"Susie, love, I'm sure you're right. Or at least I'm sure that's
how you wish things to be. But at this time of night you're letting
temptation loose. Don't you think you should put this friendship
on hold a while, perhaps see less of each other?" Dad's forehead
creased in worried lines.*

*I moved closer to him. I loved my dad and knew since I was small
how close to the Lord he lived. Scriptures and Dad went together like
seagulls and webbed feet. I didn't want to argue.*

*"Listen." He pulled me round to face him. "Will you do me and
your mum a favor? Come to church more often? Things aren't the
same without you there."*

I stared at the green carpet.

*His sigh turned into a yawn. He stood and reached out a hand to
help me up, adding, "Oh, and by the way, when you get a minute,
look up Doctrine and Covenants one thirty-two, verses fifteen and
sixteen."*

*I gave a small smile and leaned against him for a moment. "I'll
work on it," I promised.*

I turned again to the sea, dabbling my feet in the water. Icy
wavelets curled round my toes, and I arched my feet against the
tingle. Then I squirmed both heels deep into the sand before
pulling out each foot in turn, feeling the sucking squelch that left
the ground quivering. I watched, fascinated by the time it took
for the sand to return to normal.

If I left James now, I'd feel like that. It would be terrible. I
couldn't do it. We were too close and comfortable. Too many
things had been shared. Maybe marriage was the answer.

I hadn't told Dad, but I checked out that scripture he gave me. I didn't like what it said about marrying outside the temple. But surely James and I were different?

Mum brought up the same subject last week while we prepared dinner.

"Susie, before things get too serious between you and James, there's something you should think about."

I felt those here-we-go signals closing in and decided to agree instead of argue. Mum often stopped sooner that way.

"There's more to marriage than dates and fun, you know," she said.

"Yes, Mum."

"You need to pull together, share goals, and see eye-to-eye over rearing children. And then there are finances. You wouldn't believe how many marriages fall apart over finances."

"Yes, Mum."

"Do you know James's views on children?"

"Yes, Mum."

"Are they the same as yours?"

I stopped chopping carrots and put down the knife. "He has no time for children at the moment. But I'm sure when . . . I mean if we marry, we'll think along the same lines. Don't worry."

"Susie, my dear, I'm sorry, but these things are too important to not worry. There's nothing worse than having different values—you wanting babies, and him not—you wanting to save for the future, him not—you wanting to attend church, him not. It'll wrench your heart in a thousand directions."

"But love overcomes all that—right? Like in books and on TV?"

Mum sighed. "For a while, maybe." She set the salad bowl to one side then touched my arm. "Yes it does, for a little while. But I've seen marriages break under the strain. The worst part of all, if you marry a nonmember, is no spiritual closeness."

I pouted. "Oh, come on, Mum, it isn't that bad. And how about the converts? You're always telling us to be missionaries. Things work out. Besides, I can be spiritual on my own if I want."

Mum shook her head. "This may sound silly at your age, but the older you get, the more important spiritual becomes. Tugging in different directions for a long time can be miserable. And then there are the children. They get torn between the two of you."

She picked up a fresh carrot from my pile, peeling and slicing. "Think hard, my dear. Think and pray about the future. If you can't communicate about important things now, you could be in big trouble later."

My thoughts returned to the waterlogged sand. A tame gray gull with a black patch over one eye, looking like a cheeky pirate on a raid, edged forward, waiting for food. "But I love James," I told the gull. "At least I think I do. I get this amazing feeling when he looks at me, when he's next to me. But you wouldn't begin to understand, would you?"

I wandered back the way I'd come, slumping into the same sandy shelter as before, hunching my knees, clasping them tight with both hands. My head dropped forward, and the words I whispered were closer to prayer than they'd been for a long time. "Father, help me, please."

A shadow came between me and the sun. My gasp of alarm quickly turned to pleasure when I recognized the voice. It was soft and charming.

"Guessed I'd find you here," James said. "Here—grab one— they're your favorite." He dropped two Mars Bars at my feet. "Called at your house. Your mum thought you'd be here." His voice turned defensive. "She said you'd gone to think about things." He kicked puffs of sand around the base of the sea break. "So what's the deal? I want to know your answer, Susie—like now."

I bit my lip and took a deep breath. "I think I love you, James. And I think maybe it's right to—" I stopped, interrupted by the inquisitive pirate seagull sidling nearer and nearer the chocolate.

In one smooth move, James bent, grabbed a pebble, and aimed it straight at the trusting bird, yelling, "Get lost. Go find your own food. There's better fish in the sea."

Pirate gave a distressed cry, flapping his wings in fright.

"James, please don't hurt him. He . . . he's sort of a friend." I dug deep into the sand with my fingers and watched his lips twist in scornful disbelief.

"Friend! Grow up, Susie. Next you'll be telling me he brings you messages from heaven. It's only a bird. Anyway, what were you saying?"

I jumped up, clenching my fists. The words came out in a rush. "I think we should stop seeing each other." I stopped at the hurt amazement on his face, knowing I'd gone too far.

He scowled and moved toward me, his fingers curling into his palms, knuckles standing out like stones.

I backed away and raised my hand to stop him, forcing back angry tears. "Let me finish for once," I shouted. "I've discovered something. Eternal things are as important as now—maybe more so."

"Okay, okay, loosen up." James dropped his fists and raised his eyes skyward. He turned away, only to swing around and face me again. "Look, I'll be baptized this weekend if it means that much to you. How about that?"

That got to me. He looked so hopeful, and it was hard to resist the way his mouth curved in that pleading smile. At the same time, a memory pushed to the front of my mind—something a seminary teacher once said . . . about doing the right thing for the wrong reason being like not doing it at all, for all the good it did you.

I bit my lip and shook my head. "It doesn't work like that. I can't explain. We're spiritually different."

James bent and picked up another stone, flinging it far out to sea. Then he marched away, yelling over his shoulder, "Don't bother calling when you come to your senses. You won't make a fool of me twice."

The crunch of his feet on the shingle merged with the sound of dragging surf. My heart shared those wrenching tugs as each wave pulled at stubborn grit. The sun dropped behind a towering cloud. I shivered.

Picking up the chocolate bars, I set off for home, misery stretching from my throat to my stomach.

I hadn't trudged far when beating wings caught my attention. It was Pirate heading for his nest before the storm hit. This time he didn't dip and swoop in aimless fun. He was on course, flying straight and fast, strong wings taking him in the direction he needed to go.

I straightened slowly, a smile swelling inside, and called after the bird. "James was right about one thing. There *are* better fish in the sea."

My steps quickened, and I turned my face to the pouring rain letting it wash away the sadness.

Today couldn't get much worse. But tomorrow was a whole new future.

Chapter 3

Rock Bottom in a Jail Cell

(Exeter, Devon, England)

Alex Styles drummed his fingers on the metal table in the gloomy visiting hall of Exeter prison. He kept his head down, avoiding eye contact with Bishop Watson and his counselor, Brother Hill, sitting across from him on the opposite side of the table.

"We'd like to help you, Alex," the bishop said.

Alex mumbled. "I don't need help." What was one more lie among so many? He wasn't even sure what truth was any more.

Matt Hill cleared his throat and added, "Your family misses you . . . especially that little sister of yours, Linda. She looks so lost when I see her at church every Sunday. They all love you, Alex."

Alex lowered his head until his forehead rested on his arms. Family was the last thing he wanted to hear about. *Why don't these men go home? They've been here over an hour already. This isn't Sunday School. No amount of preaching can help me now. Don't they realize that none of this applies to me anymore?*

Maybe if I can be sick, they'll leave. He tried to gag, half rising to his feet.

But Bishop Watson's soft voice kept droning on. Alex risked a glance at their faces and was surprised to see they too were looking down. He sank back in his chair, watching through half-closed eyes, ready to duck his head the minute they looked up. The bishop seemed tired and old, his normally slick grey hair untidy. Matt Hill slumped forward, elbows resting on the table, head in hands, long fingers stuck in his sandy hair like two chunky hair combs.

Alex flicked his long hair to one side. It was brown, the lank strands greasy because washing it was too much trouble. Someone once told him he looked like Johnny Depp, but Alex knew better. *If I did, I wouldn't be locked away in here.*

The bishop was still rambling on. Alex rolled his eyes. Maybe they could keep him here, but he didn't have to listen.

His mind drifted back to his sixteenth birthday. Was it really only a year since this whole drug nightmare began? No, it went further back than that . . . to Devin's house after school the summer they both turned fourteen.

Some friend Devin turned out to be. Alex saw it all as if it were yesterday.

They were sitting at Devin's kitchen table comparing homework. Devin went to the fridge and pulled out two cans of beer then returned to sit at the table.

"Come on, Alex," Devin held out a can. Alex shook his head. Devin's voice was full of scorn. "Don't be such a wuss. You must be the only one in class who's never tried beer. Can't be bad if it makes you feel great, now can it?"

Alex turned away. Devin should know better. There weren't many young men in Exeter Ward, and they'd all heard about the Word of Wisdom since Primary. Just because Devin's dad wasn't a member didn't mean Devine had to follow his dad's beer habits.

Devin grabbed Alex's arm and shoved the drink at him again. "Do you think I don't know how stressed out you get? We're all the same. School piles on the homework like we're machines."

Alex sighed. It was true. And on top of everything, Mum and Dad expected him to get good report cards, and be as perfect as his older brother, Ryan—now on a mission. Some joke. Alex couldn't memorize scriptures in seminary, and was always bottom of the class at school. What a loser. All he did well was play the guitar. And as Dad so often said, "That's fine for a hobby, but don't count on it for a living."

He rubbed his temples. What was he supposed to do about this drink? Without Devin, he'd have no friends. Alex was the third of seven children, with a sister immediately older and one younger. They had their own friends. His family never talked about situations like the one he was in right now. Maybe trying alcohol this once wouldn't hurt, and it would get Devin off his back.

Alex wavered. "It might taste weird."

"You'll get used to it. You know what? I read on the Internet that five out of ten fourteen-year-olds in Utah have tried alcohol." Devin banged the can on the table, nudging it toward Alex. "Can't have Utah Mormons beating us, now can we?"

"How do you know they're Mormons?"

"How do you know they're not? That's where Mormons live, isn't it?"

"Some of them. There must be other people there."

"Whatever." Devin popped his can and slurped beer. Then he grabbed the second drink, flipped the ring tab, and plunked the can in front of Alex. "Go on. Try it."

At first, Alex sat there fingering the shiny metal, staring at the bubbles frothing over the side. Then, he pulled the can to his nose and sniffed the contents. Would it hurt to take one sip? It was a hot day after all, and he was thirsty.

The ice cold fizz pulled him in.

That was when it all began. The next time was easier. Then came cigarettes. And within a few months they'd moved on to marijuana. One day that autumn, Devin introduced mushrooms to the mix. Months later, they found themselves obsessed with hallucinogenics and began combining drugs of every kind.

Devin took Alex round the back of his garage after school. "Got some Special K," he said, drawing white powder in a plastic bag from his trouser pocket. "You'll forget the world with this one."

Alex pulled back. "I'm okay with the other stuff. Don't need anything stronger."

"You soon will. Try this. You won't be sorry."

"But what if we're found out?"

"No one's guessed so far, have they?"

"They don't notice what I'm doing at home most of the time."

"So what's your problem?"

Alex ground his heel into the dirt. "I'm scared of getting hooked, that's what."

Devin laughed. "Too late for that."

"No way! I can stop whenever I want" Alex shook his head. "I couldn't handle addiction. It would be embarrassing if anyone thought . . . I mean, if they knew. You know . . . at church and—"

Devin interrupted. "I don't think about it any more. It's my life, and I can do what I want with it."

"What about family?"

"With Mum and Dad working, they're only around evenings and weekends, and then it's chores and more chores. They're glad I'm out of the way. They don't care what I do."

"I think mine care . . . especially little Linda."

He'd gone home and spent two hours in his room that night, playing the guitar to take his mind off things.

Alex heard his name and sat up with a start, the scent of disinfectant floor wash reminding him where he was. He slouched back on the wooden chair staring at Bishop Watson. How much longer did he have to sit here? It was all a waste of time. Hopeless. His life was over.

"Did you hear me, Alex?" the bishop asked.

"What?"

"I said you have to trust me."

Alex let out a harsh laugh. "I don't trust anyone anymore. Not myself, not anyone."

The two men rose from their seats looking sad and drained. They glanced at each other, then the bishop turned back to Alex. "We care about you, Alex. And we can help. But you have to want it bad enough to fight for your life."

They pushed back their chairs, scraping them across the hard wood floor, adding more clatter to the already buzzing room. Then they returned the chairs neatly under the table edge and left, their footsteps echoing down the long passageway to freedom. Alex covered his face with his hands and let the tears go.

That night, in the loneliness of his bleak cell, the past kept him awake for hours.

Of course he'd listened to Devin . . . and tried the white powder . . . and that's when life turned into a spiraling nightmare. They found someone selling ecstasy, and by early spring they were so dependant on the vibe that nothing in life seemed worth doing without the high from this drug.

Mum suspected something. She kept looking at him like he was important all of a sudden—not a good kind of important. It was one Wednesday night when they all got home from Mutual that she opened up.

"Is everything all right, Alex?"

"Yep."

"You've been quieter than normal lately."

"Umm."

"Someone said they'd seen you and Devin taking pills behind the cycle sheds at school last week."

"Nope. Not me."

"They described you perfectly . . . your green jacket and khaki backpack."

"Others have green jackets. It's the style."

"You'd tell me if you had a problem, wouldn't you?"

"Yep."

"Well . . . I want to trust you."

Relief swamped Alex as he went to his room. So . . . she'd not noticed the money missing from her purse. That meant he could still get cash. It was scary stealing from the local store. But they trusted him, too, and that made it easier when he had to do it. Finding drug money was getting more and more difficult.

Next Wednesday night Mum nabbed him again . . . at the very minute everyone was out of the car and into the house. They had the garage to themselves. This time, worry lines creased Mum's forehead, and it seemed like she was about to burst with stress.

"Alex. I don't want to believe this, but Devin's mother told me tonight that he has a problem. A huge problem." She bit her lip. "Are you . . . did you know he's doing drugs?"

Alex froze. Should he tell more lies, or should he confess? He couldn't stand seeing Mum hurt. And what about Dad? Was he onto him, too? Whichever way he went meant deep trouble.

He flung open the car door and jumped out, escaping through the side garage door into the front garden. Ignoring Mum's frantic shouts, he leapt over a hedge onto the pavement and raced toward town, running down side streets and taking short cuts until his lungs wouldn't pump any more.

He collapsed, panting, onto a small stone wall surrounding a run-down Victorian house in the old part of Exeter town.

Alex glanced around and wrung his hands. It was dark and spooky. He didn't know this place with drab boarded-up windows and scary creaks and groans. He pressed his hands against his stomach, trying to stop the violent trembling that threatened to overpower his whole body. If he didn't get a fix soon, he'd go crazy. But he didn't have his stuff with him.

He ground his teeth. He had to get to his room and pick up his stash from its secret place—an old black shoe under the bed. Going home was his only option. But he didn't dare risk it until the family was asleep. How could he survive another two hours?

Alex jumped up and walked on through the back streets of the city, avoiding people and barking dogs. By midnight, he'd almost blacked out twice. He couldn't stand the craving any longer. Starting for home, his head burned, and he wanted to vomit so bad he could barely stay upright. If he didn't get the drug soon, he'd fall apart.

The front porch light was on when he arrived. Alex caught his breath. Were they expecting him? He'd best be careful. He couldn't get caught. Not now. Not minutes away from a fix.

He crept round the back entrance and fumbled for the latch on the garden gate. Good. No light from the kitchen window. He reached up to the ledge above the back door where Mum kept the spare key, his fingers fumbling in the dust until they closed round cold metal.

The key turned quietly in the lock. Alex crept into the dark house. He was on the first stair when Dad's voice made his heart jump so hard it took his breath away.

"We have to talk, Alex. Come into the lounge."

"But, it's late, and—"

"This is important, son. Mum and I waited up for you."

Alex tossed and turned on his narrow prison bed, reliving

the anguish of that night. Mum got hysterical when she saw the desperate state he was in. Dad's lecturing made things more painful. Brothers and sisters appeared on the stairs, listening in sleepy bewilderment to the racket below.

In total sorrow, they ended up letting him get his fix that night. The next day, they found him a place in a treatment center. It was all hushed up . . . the family sworn to secrecy, pretending nothing bad was going on.

When Alex returned from rehab, Mum and Dad thought he was cured, and things slowly returned to normal. Family life went on its usual noisy way, and everyone tried to forget there was ever a problem.

But Alex remained stable for a few months only.

Devin came home from rehab several weeks after Alex and phoned that weekend.

"Got any E?" was the first thing he asked.

"You must be joking. Why would I want to go through all that again?"

"Because the same problems are still out there, and you can't deal with them. And because you know you can't live without it, and that means you'll most likely die by the time you're twenty." He sniggered. "So why not die high in our magical world?" He laughed again. "Know what? The more I think about getting a fix, the more I want it. You too?"

Alex didn't answer. Instead, he said, "I'll meet you at the chippy in half an hour."

The downward spiral began again. Only this time, things were far worse.

Alex gave up trying to sleep on the prison bed. He'd lost so much weight that his skin was covered in sores where bones rubbed against the hard mattress and coarse sheets. The sores matched the infected needle punctures on his arms.

He was cold, and his head ached. Loneliness clamped down on him with a vicious grip. Misery gave way to despair as morning light filtered in through the tiny square window near the stone ceiling. If he could die, all this would go away . . . or would it? Wasn't he damned for eternity?

He hated himself for getting into such a mess. If only he'd had more sense. If only he'd gone to the bishop at the beginning—or Mum and Dad. If only he'd kept away from Devin. It hadn't taken long before their crushing need for money led to bigger and more daring crimes.

By this time, his parents knew things were bad, but they seemed helpless and unable to deal with it. Were they living in some kind of dream world where everything works out right in the end? It was all so stupid. His life was terrible, but he was powerless to change. Shame and fear chewed on his mind. The drugs had taken over. He was no longer in control.

The old cheerful atmosphere at home was now weighed down with anxiety, shouting, depression, and suspicion—like someone had switched off the light.

Devin came to Alex's house in a panic one Sunday when everyone was at church.

"Joe has the stuff we need," Devin said. "But he's upped the price. We have to get the money to him by tomorrow night or we're finished."

Alex's eyelids started twitching. It was something he couldn't stop these days. "Dad's cheque book might be in his room."

Devin punched air. "Yes! Can you forge his signature?"

"How do you think I get sick notes signed for school?"

"Well, what are we waiting for?"

"He could have hidden it. They don't trust me any more."

Devin gave a wild laugh. "Wonder why?"

They'd found the cheque book buried among Dad's underpants in a drawer. Alex wrote a cheque, payable to himself, for one thousand pounds. Next day, they took it to the bank. That's when life changed from bad to unbearable in a matter of hours.

The cashier took their cheque to another room, and Alex heard a different voice talking on the phone.

"Mr. Styles? This is Jack Cooper, the manager at—"

Alex didn't wait for more. He grabbed Devin by the arm, and the two of them forced their way into the manager's office, pulling out knives as they went.

Mr. Cooper dropped the phone, reaching for a button on his desk.

In panic, Alex tried to stop the man from hitting the alarm, but by mistake slashed Mr. Cooper's wrist. Blood spurted in red splats onto the posh green carpet.

The shock brought Alex to his knees.

Devin hauled on his arm, screaming, "Run!"

But Alex couldn't move. He knelt there, staring at the blood. Mr. Cooper's moans sounded far away. The next moment, sirens blared, tires screeched, and voices yelled—the terrifying sounds swirling around his head like angry bees.

The manager survived the cut artery and later bore witness— along with both sets of parents—at Alex and Devin's trial.

Now here he was a prisoner in Exeter Jail.

Alex turned to the cell wall and beat upon it with tight fists until the walls were smeared with blood.

How could his parents witness against him? So much for love. So much for anything they'd ever taught him. On top of that, enforced withdrawal from drugs inside prison was more dreadful than anything he'd ever experienced. He couldn't go on any longer.

Alex dragged through that day in constant pain, both physical and mental. He watched for anything that could be used to take his own life. But there was nothing. He might have guessed. How many others had wished the same in this awful Victorian building?

That night he was in no mood for visitors—especially not the bishop—but there he was, sitting once more on the other side of the metal table, smiling that warm smile that no amount of coldness from Alex could wipe away.

"Alex, my friend. Brother Hill can't be here tonight, so you've got me to yourself." His eyes narrowed. "How are things?"

Alex yawned. What kind of stupid question was that? There was no answer he could possibly give that this man would understand.

Bishop Watson leaned forward. "Don't worry. I can guess. You must be pretty much at rock bottom by now. Right?"

Alex shrugged and let his empty stare drift upward to the high, arched ceiling.

"It's okay, Alex. You don't need to answer. I'm good with silence. If you want to listen, then that's okay, too."

Alex looked down, shaking his head. Was there really any choice?

Then the bishop asked an odd question that brought Alex up sharp.

"How would you like to hear some remarkable music?"

Alex frowned, picturing an orchestra. Classical wasn't his scene. But he did miss his guitar. "What kind of music?"

"There's a CD I've heard, called *Wings of Glory*—young people's music. It's helping substance abuse victims."

Alex shrugged again, faking disinterest. They probably wouldn't allow a CD in here anyway.

The bishop continued as if reading Alex's mind. "I can get permission for you to hear it in rehab, if you like." He stood. "Have to go now. Promised my wife I'd be home for dinner. Let me know."

He was off his chair and heading for the door before Alex replied. As the visiting hall door creaked open, Alex called out, "I'd . . . like that."

Whether Bishop Watson heard or not through all the noise, he couldn't tell.

Next day, the bishop came in his lunch hour and handed a CD to the prison officer who brought Alex to the table.

Alex's eyes brightened.

Bishop Watson pulled out a chair and sat. "When they play that for you, really listen to the words. If you're short on hope, those songs can make a difference."

Alex's eyes clouded over. He dropped into his chair. "Hope isn't a word I use any more."

"It might be all you need right now."

"I don't think so." Alex shifted in his chair. Why was he even bothering to reply? He'd already decided that not speaking got rid of do-gooders faster than answering. But then . . . the bishop did bring a CD.

Alex shot a quick glance at the elderly man opposite. He looked like Linda on Christmas morning, with that expectant, blue-eyed stare. Okay. So give him five minutes.

Bishop Watson was still speaking. "You don't know? Hope is a major part of repentance."

Alex burst out, "Like repentance is an option? After all I've done, repentance flew out the window—along with forgiveness and everything else." He thumped the desk top with his fist, raising his voice. "I might as well keep doing drugs and commit any crime I want when I get out, because it won't make any difference."

The bishop's eyebrows shot up. "My goodness! No wonder you have no hope. If I believed that for one minute, I'd be hopeless too. Of course you can be forgiven. That's the whole glorious miracle of the Saviour's life . . . and His death."

Alex wriggled in his chair, pushing away a fluttery feeling in his chest.

Bishop Watson added, "He loves you more than you can imagine—especially right now." His voice became gentle but firm. "Forgiveness doesn't come without pain and hard work, but believe me, it *can* come. It brings peace to the tormented soul."

Alex saw tears in Bishop Watson's eyes, and for one startling moment it was as if the Saviour looked right out. It triggered something locked deep inside Alex's own soul. He coughed on unexpected emotion. Then he took a long, shuddering breath and whispered, "Is it . . . possible? Is it really possible?"

"You bet it's possible. Like I said—listen to the words on that CD with your heart switched on. The person who wrote them knows where you're coming from because her own son traveled the same agonizing road as you—and made it. She calls recovery a natural high."

The bishop pulled a small book from his trouser pocket and flipped through the pages. "She wrote something else." He began to read, his deep voice penetrating Alex's cloudy mind with sharp bursts of fire.

"'Your personal agony may break your wings as you struggle with your own addictions and compulsive behaviors. But hold onto hope. You *will* fly once again someday—*on your own wings of glory.*'"

Alex blinked back tears, shaken by the warm feeling rushing through his chest in waves.

Then he bowed his head and wept.

AUTHOR'S NOTE:

I'm indebted to Kristine Litster Fales, and her son, Jonathan Fales, for support and advice so generously given to help this story be accurate. Kristine is married to David Fales, and they are parents of eleven children. Their oldest son, Jonathan, is no longer abusing drugs and alcohol but actively promotes the Word of Wisdom and healthy behavior. He credits the Odyssey House of Salt Lake City, Utah, for teaching him the behavior modification and life skills he uses today. More details can be found at:

http://www.odysseyhouse.org/

Kristine Fales says, "*Wings of Glory: Hope and Healing from Addiction* is a collection of songs and stories inspired by experiences in my own family. They reflect the sorrow, the hope, and the healing that can come from addiction. These songs and stories are not only for people who suffer from the disease of addiction, but also for their families and friends."

Kristine can be contacted as follows:
Email: info@falesproductions.com
Telephone: 1-877-434-HOPE (4673)
Website: www.WingsOfGlory.net

Chapter 4

Advertised on Her Face

(Culloden, Inverness, Scotland)

Elder Kalan Ballantyne shifted in his seat and tapped his foot. As they landed at Inverness Airport, the cloud cover blocked all view of Scotland's Highlands. But it didn't matter. He was nearly home. Home, family, and Gemma. After two long years, he could finally let Gemma into his thoughts. They'd agreed not to even write after he'd been gone twelve months so he could give his whole attention to the work.

An elderly woman in a tweed skirt sitting next to him interrupted his thoughts. "Are we there, laddie?"

"We certainly are. Inverness at last." He let out a long and happy sigh, settling once more to dreams of Gemma—brown hair waving across her face, her large brown eyes and laughing mouth.

"Och! Have I slept all the way from Heathrow?" The lady peered at Kalan as if seeing him for the first time, then pushed her glasses firmly on her nose. "You a visitor then, laddie? I'm Mrs. McKivett, by the way. I can't quite place your accent."

Kalan brushed a hand over his cropped brown hair and chuckled. "Not exactly a visitor. I've been in Switzerland for two years doing missionary work for my church. My accent's a mixture of German, French, American, and Scottish by now."

She smiled, nodding. "Ahh! That explains everything."

Before he could ask what *everything* meant, the airplane taxied to a halt, and the confusion of leaving the aircraft began.

Kalan saw his parents as soon as the baggage cleared. With them was sixteen-year-old Adam, now taller than himself, at least six feet—and eleven-year-old Beth, a wide grin on her face, skipping around the three of them. With a lump in his throat, he reached out to meet their embraces. He gazed from face to familiar face. He felt complete, like his mission had crowned them all with a circle of love.

But part of the circle was missing.

"Is Gemma working or something?" he asked his mother as soon as the questions and answers slowed down.

Kalan thought he saw dismay on her face before she glanced away. He caught his breath.

"Let's get home first, dear," she whispered. "Then we'll talk."

The drive to Culloden village took forever. Kalan tried to concentrate on the scenery instead of Gemma as they sped over bridges and down winding roads. A view of the Firth winding down to the sea appeared now and again between frosted hillsides. It was shrouded in mist. His replies to the family became automatic.

His father leaned across, patting his arm. "Don't worry, son. You must be exhausted. We'll get you in the house, then you can take a nap before tonight's party. It was going to be here, but so many people wanted to come that President Watson said we could use the cultural hall."

When they got home, and Kalan had rediscovered his old room, he was too preoccupied to sleep. He unpacked a few things then ran downstairs to find his mother. Following delicious smells of home-made cake, he found her in the kitchen, her face spotted with flour. How he'd missed her and the comforting mood of her kitchen. But Mum was far from comfortable. Her look shouted bad news before she spoke.

"I'm sorry, dear." Her placid face broke into small lines of worry, and she struggled for words.

Kalan heart thumped. "Gemma . . . she's not sick, is she?"

"No. It's not that. Gemma is . . . we would have written, but we didn't want to spoil things for you before your return."

"She's found someone else, hasn't she?" Kalan stared out the window, anguish squeezing his chest. He cleared his throat. "Is she happy? What's he like? Is he a member? How long—? "

"It's best you see for yourself tonight." Sister Ballantyne put an arm around her son. "Go and rest, Kalan. You'll feel better after a sleep."

He returned to his room and fell on the bed, sleep now further away than ever. His future always held Gemma. Even though she stayed in a distant corner of his thoughts for two years, he couldn't imagine life with anyone else.

His thoughts became a prayer, which turned into a hymn they'd sung at the last zone conference before his mission ended. That conference was the first time Kalan had noticed the song in the hymnbook. Now here it was in clear replay. "School thy feelings, O my brother; Train thy warm, impulsive soul. Do not its emotions smother, but let wisdom's voice control . . ."

Kalan jumped off the bed, rummaging through his backpack until his fingers touched a familiar book. The pages flipped open, and a sheet of paper dropped out. The mission president had given everyone the same quote that day: "What a man thinks in his heart, he advertises on his face."

He gave a quiet chuckle and decided he wouldn't spoil this homecoming for anyone. Somehow he would smile at them all. He sighed, then flopped on the bed, relaxing in the luxury of being home. Sleep eventually came.

* * *

A few hours later, Kalan was glad he'd rested. The cultural hall was packed by the time the Stake President officially released him. Members, family, old school friends—everyone was there.

Kalan worked his way around the crowd and stopped in amazement at the sight of a familiar face.

"Well, laddie, I thought I'd find you here. Remember me?"

"Of course." Kalan blinked at the elderly lady from the plane, still in the same tweed skirt. "I'd no idea you were LDS."

"LDS? Never heard of it. They called me an investigator last week. My name's Eva McKivett , but not to worry." She hooked her hand through his elbow, steering him toward a seat at the back of the hall. Kalan's stomach knotted when he saw where they were heading. There was no escape. Next to the empty chairs sat Gemma and her new boyfriend.

"I have genuine respect for you young Elders," Eva continued. "Taught me a few things this past month. Must say, I like what I hear." She turned an unwavering gaze on Kalan.

"Now then . . ." She eyed his missionary badge. "Now then, Elder Ballantyne, please point out your mother and father to me. They've done a fine job raising you. And then tell me which of these pretty wee lassies waited for you to come home." She tapped his arm, blue eyes twinkling behind the glasses.

By now Kalan was squirming. He'd caught Gemma's eye before sitting down, but on hearing her sudden intake of breath at Mrs. McKivett's question, didn't dare turn in her direction.

"My parents are over there by the Branch President." He spoke fast, half standing, hoping she'd follow. "I'll introduce you to them."

"No, no, laddie, not yet. Only just sat down." She pulled him onto his chair again, surveying the handful of young women scattered around the hall. "So which one—?"

"Excuse me." The voice was curt.

Kalan let out his breath with relief at the interruption—until he realized it came from the young man next to Gemma.

"Duncan's the name, Duncan Munroe. Gemma made me come tonight. We might as well get this over with." The young man extended one hand to Kalan, slapping him on the shoulder with the other.

While Kalan introduced Mrs. McKivett, he took stock of Duncan. The light red hair and fair complexion, so typical of Highlanders, gave Duncan a distinctive air—and he was well over six feet tall.

Kalan stood and turned to Gemma. As their eyes met, he was puzzled by what he saw, but the odd expression was gone in a second. She gave him a false-looking smile, holding out her hand. "Welcome home, Kalan. It's good to see you again. I've missed you. Your mission went quicker than I expected."

Kalan shook her hand. This didn't feel right. He wanted to give her a long hug. "Quicker than you can imagine," he said.

"Och, Gemma." Duncan grabbed her hand, hauling her to her feet. "That's about as much missionary talk as I can take for one night. You'll not catch me taking off for two years and leaving my woman behind." He laughed and pulled Gemma to his other side, away from Kalan, before they moved away.

Kalan caught a glimpse of Gemma's blush and look of distress. His stomach churned, but he gave her a quick wink.

Someone poked his arm. He'd forgotten Mrs. McKivett.

"Ah ha!" she said, head nodding. "So that's the one." She pulled on Kalan's jacket until he sat once more, then continued. "I think it's time to turn the tables. Let me be teacher for a moment, and you be . . . what's the word . . . the investigator?" She sounded bossy, but her kindly smile made up for it.

Kalan winced. "Whatever you say."

"Do you love this lassie?"

"Yes."

"Then what are you going to do about it?"

The question took him by surprise. "Uh . . . I guess I could go away . . . far away—back to Switzerland maybe."

"Is that what you really want?"

"Of course not."

"Is that what she really wants?"

"I'm thinking she knows her own mind."

"Are they engaged?"

"Couldn't see a ring."

"Then what are you waiting for? My father always said, 'If what you want is right, then don't give up until it's yours.'"

"Sounds like he should have been a missionary," Kalan said, sending her a fleeting grin.

"I'm not against eejits—they have their place—but to my way of thinking, that bonny lass deserves better." She eased to her feet. "Now you go find her before it's too late." She shooed him away and walked toward his parents.

It was an hour later before Kalan escaped the crowd and found a peaceful moment on his own in the chapel. There'd been no chance to search for Gemma. He sank into a seat by the wall and shut his eyes. It was good to be home, but he missed having a companion for talking things through.

He thought about Mrs. McKivett. What if she was wrong? Suppose Gemma really loved Duncan? He couldn't go all out to break up a relationship that might bring her happiness. Kalan reached for a hymnbook and skipped through several pages before he realized someone had entered the chapel.

Gemma whispered, "May I join you?"

For a second, Kalan was too stunned to move. He didn't know if he wanted this conversation. Then Mrs. McKivett's parting remarks echoed in his mind. He nodded at Gemma.

"I . . . I'm sorry about Duncan." She perched on the bench a couple of feet from him.

"You don't need to apologize. You're a free person. Always were."

"When you and I stopped writing, he wouldn't stay away. He's very persuasive, you know."

"I noticed."

"We got engaged last week." She looked down at her fingers. "No ring. Duncan can't afford one."

Kalan turned away. He told himself to keep cool, keep smiling—let her think he didn't mind.

"But," she went on with a rush, "I only agreed because he said I owed him after dating for a year."

"You mean . . . you aren't in love with him?"

"I don't know. I thought I was . . . until . . ." She stared at Kalan with sad eyes. "I don't expect you to understand. And I don't expect us to be where we were before. I simply want to—" She broke off, turning her face away.

It was then Kalan noticed the bruise on her cheek. He gasped and reached out his hand, then withdrew it slowly. Gemma's chin dropped, and he heard the tremor in her voice.

"In the car park, I told Duncan I wanted to go back to the party. He got angrier than he ever has before."

Kalan touched her arm. "Gemma, listen to me—"

"Gemma," Duncan's tight voice sounded from the back of the chapel. He cleared his throat. "It's time to go."

Gemma jumped, her eyes wide. She scooted off the seat and ran up the aisle to Duncan's side. He took her arm and led her out the door.

Kalan rubbed his face, not sure what to do. He didn't want to make things worse for Gemma, but if he didn't do something, the man might hurt her some more. He made a snap decision. Whether she loved Duncan or not, he had to go after them.

Kalan shot from the bench and out of the chapel. He heard the heavy doors at the front of the building swing shut. Duncan must be in some hurry to get out that fast. By the time Kalan opened the door and looked outside, they were no longer in sight.

Then he heard fierce swearing and raced around the corner of the chapel toward the sound.

"You're ne'er to see him again, you little two-timer. D'ya hear me?"

Gemma's hands covered her face. She was sobbing.

Duncan moved closer to her, his arm swinging up, fists ready.

Kalan covered the last few yards and leaped for Duncan's legs, knocking him to the ground before the blow could land. Duncan kicked and struggled, twisting into a sitting position, reaching for Kalan's arms. His fist thudded into Kalan's wrist, sending pain shooting through the bones. But Kalan didn't let go. Instead, he used Duncan's ankles to pull himself upright, and heaved, toppling the taller man sideways.

Kalan stood and stepped back. Duncan scrambled to his feet and was about to run at Kalan when Gemma stepped between them. Her eyes were wide, and she panted like a scared animal. But her small chin came up, and she stayed in place.

"Stop it!" Her head swung back and forth between the two men. "You'll not harm each other because of me."

Duncan brushed at dirt clinging to his jeans and spat on the ground. "Then don't let me catch you with Mr. Religion, or you'll not stop me next time." He took Gemma's wrist.

She flinched at his touch, and Kalan couldn't bear it. He shouted, "That's enough. Let her go, and I'll keep away. But I'll tell you something, and you'd better listen—God wants her treated with respect."

Duncan sneered. "Och, so now you speak for God?"

"Abusing women is not God's way. It never was. Gemma deserves so much more."

"Mind your own business, you blethering eejit." Duncan let go of Gemma and clenched his fists, moving again toward Kalan.

Kalan stood his ground, his head high. "She is my business. I still love her—even if she's chosen someone else."

Duncan stopped and frowned. "You mean you'll not come between her and me?"

"Gemma's free to choose. But I'm coming after you if you hurt her again."

"Huh." Duncan shoved his hands in his pockets, glancing across at Gemma. She bit her lip, not looking at either of them, tears sliding down her cheeks. She took a step closer to Duncan, hesitated, shot a despairing look at Kalan, then turned and ran toward the chapel.

Kalan heard the doors squeak shut. He waited for Duncan to make a move, but the man stood there, scratching his head. Unexpectedly, Kalan felt sorry for him. Duncan looked both puzzled and weak, despite his size. The uncertainty in the man's eyes disappeared when Kalan held out a hand.

Duncan smashed it away. "I'm going after her, and you'd better not follow."

Kalan let him go. He wandered down the busy main road for half an hour, then headed toward the chapel once more. It was cold out, and he was tired of dwelling on his loss. He stopped at the edge of the chapel car park and straightened his trousers, then rubbed off mud from his jacket sleeve. He was about to find his parents and persuade them to go home, when he noticed someone leaving the building.

Gemma appeared first, followed by President Watson. No sign of Duncan. The President stopped and shook Gemma's hand, then they walked a few yards closer to the cars, talking, their voices carrying on the frosty air.

"Thanks so much, President Watson. What you've told me makes all the difference."

He patted her arm. "It may be difficult for a while, but we'll find a way through this, even if we have to involve the police. However, after tonight, I don't think it will come to that." He stopped again and turned toward the chapel, calling over his shoulder. "Now go find Elder Ballantyne and make his day."

Kalan's heart leapt. He took a step forward. She saw him and quickened her pace. They met in the middle of the car park and stood gazing at each other.

Gemma spoke first. "It's all right, Kalan."

"I know. I heard. You can't imagine how glad I am you're safe."

"I'm so very sorry. I made a terrible mistake." She reached out her hand and touched his fingers.

Kalan pulled her toward him, lifting her chin with one hand. He waited until Gemma's warm brown eyes met his, and then smiled a long, tender smile. "Mistakes are part of life," he said. "It's how we fix them that matters. And I think the fixing is advertised on your face."

Chapter 5

Someteen Going on Umpteen

(Spanish Fork, Utah, USA)

Kacie couldn't believe what she'd done. *Why does it always happen to me?* The words came out too fast, too messed up. *Lucas will never speak to me again.*

She ran the two blocks home from church, wishing it was a dark winter night. Being mid-summer, all the neighbors could see her tears, and Dad was bound to be in the front yard. If only she could go back an hour and start over. Never again would she tell Lucas—tall, hunky, every-girl's-dream-date, seventeen-year-old Lucas Harvey—"Don't even think of being a doctor. You look more like a builder than any doctor I know."

The others laughed, but Lucas's tanned face turned crimson, and his blue eyes looked like slits of ice. He walked away, hands jammed in his jeans pockets. She was joking, of course. All she meant to say was how much she admired his abs that came from helping his dad build houses on weekends. But that wasn't how it sounded, and now she'd ruined everything

Kacie slowed her pace and brushed away tears. Sure enough, her dad was weeding borders, whistling something tuneless. She put on a grin. "Hey! Yard looks nice."

"You're home early." He smiled and threw her a dandelion. "Meeting no good?"

Kacie caught the flower and began peeling off yellow petals. "It was fine." She shrugged. "Had enough, is all."

Dad dug between two rose bushes, lifting out long strings of Morning Glory. "Sure nothing's wrong?"

She tossed strands of brown hair over one shoulder. "Nothing's right, more like."

"Want to talk about it?"

"Nope. Talking got me in enough trouble for one night."

Dad kept on digging. "Suit yourself, kiddo. Don't stew too long."

She waved and kept walking across sun-baked grass toward the house, dropping thin petals as she went.

Wednesday was Mom's Book Club night, so the house was empty. Though right now, Kacie wished her older brother, Mike, was home from his mission. She missed his friendship. He always seemed to understand her problems, and she ached for his advice. The other three siblings had married and moved out before Mike left.

Okay, so what would Mike do? He'd laugh, that's what, and tell me to go apologize. The thought made Kacie cringe. No way. She couldn't face Lucas again. Not ever.

She opened the back door, wandered through the kitchen, grabbed a glass from the shelf, and then looked in the refrigerator for something cold. Nothing—not even a carton of milk. Wonderful! Warm tap water was all she needed to make this night perfect.

Then she remembered something else. The road show. The Young Men and Young Women leaders had decided to rehash something fun for the summer from the old days. They'd written an updated version of *The Sound of Music*, only they called it *The Sound of Mutual*. And Kacie was chosen to play Liesl von Trapp to Lucas's Rolfe. The names had been changed too—to Weasel von Flap and Wolf.

That which had brought a song to her lips since last week, no longer made her smile. She couldn't rehearse night after night with Lucas after what happened. Someone else would have to take her part and . . . oh no! . . . kiss Wolf! The kiss was just a peck on the cheek in the new script, but it was enough to melt her bones.

Kacie dabbed at tears sliding down her cheeks. She'd practiced *I Am Someteen Going on Umpteen* every day. And tonight, when they'd all gone over the script for the first time, the look in Lucas's eyes when they sang their song took her breath away. Oh, why did she have to go and spoil everything?

Later that night Kacie lay in bed wide awake. Her brain wouldn't stop running over the whole impossible conversation with Lucas. Poor Lucas. What if she'd ruined his life, and he never became a doctor? Whenever she saw him pouring concrete in the future, she would drown in guilt. She'd have to move far away so she didn't see his misery—forever in a job he didn't want, forever wishing for something he couldn't have. And he would have made a wonderful doctor. Really, he would.

She tossed around, throwing off the sheet, trying to cool down. After kicking thoughts around for another half hour, she realized she'd forgotten her prayers. She rolled onto the floor beside the bed, head in hands, pleading for Lucas to get his self confidence back. Then she flopped back into bed.

She must have slept, because the last time she looked at the clock it was two o'clock in the morning. Now daylight poked into the room through cracks in the blind. Memories of last night at church came in with the sun, and she shuddered. She tumbled out of bed wondering who to call first—the Young Women's President or Sister Shelly, the road show producer?

When she looked in the mirror and saw her puffy brown eyes and swollen lower lip, she did neither. If only she could climb back into bed and stay there all day. But that was impossible. She'd promised to baby-sit for Sister Parry this morning, and was working at Albertsons in Spanish Fork in the afternoon.

She picked up her hairbrush and tipped her head forward, brushing with long strokes. Then she fumbled for a hair band, tying a ponytail high on her head, letting the mass of dark brown curls fall over her shoulders. Finally she went to the bathroom and splashed her face with cold water to tone down the blotchy skin.

Kacie dragged through the day, her mind never far away from the Big Lucas Mess. It settled like an enormous zit right in the middle of her thoughts.

By five o'clock she was tired, hot, and ready to drop. Only one more hour, and she still hadn't decided what to do about tonight's rehearsal at Sister Shelly's home. She glanced around. At last—no one in the checkout line. She leaned against the counter and shut her eyes, letting her body go limp. Then she gasped as someone tapped her head, and familiar laughter brought her eyes flying open.

"Hey! Weasel. You in there?"

"Ah . . . yes . . . oh, Lucas . . . ?" Kacie shot upright, feeling the blood rush to her face. "I . . . I'm so sorry for . . . you know—"

"That's okay. Forget it."

"But I didn't say it right last night. Your dad made a strong worker out of you . . . I mean, you're so muscular—you'll make a great kiss—I mean, a great Wolf." Kacie's hands flew to her mouth at the exasperated look on Lucas's face.

He shook his head, placed the bottle of water he carried on the counter without paying, and walked out.

Kacie's knees shook. She wanted to scream. Another customer dumped groceries to her left, and she picked them up in a daze, punching buttons like a robot, scanning item after item, trying not to cry.

She had to get over this. It was ruining her life. She picked up Lucas's water and set it under the counter next to her purse. She'd take it to him tonight, and apologize properly . . . even if the words didn't come out the way she wanted. Then she'd walk away, head in the air.

At last six o'clock arrived, and Kacie handed over the register to the next girl. She grabbed her things and paid for Lucas's bottled water, then walked into the sizzling parking lot for the long trek home. The sun was blinding, and she didn't notice who it was standing there at first. But she quickly dropped her hand from her eyes at the sound of his deep voice.

"Weasel von Flap. Couldn't have picked a better part for you—the Flap thing, I mean. You sure get into big trouble flapping that cute mouth."

For a minute, she didn't know if he was being mean or laughing at her. He sounded so stern. She risked a glance at his face and sighed with relief. His blue eyes had lost their coldness.

She fell into step beside him, working out how to say sorry. Again.

He walked faster. "I've been thinking about what you said." He held up his hand as she tried to speak.

"Your brother Mike and I used to hang out before his mission. We laughed over things you told him—mistakes you made."

Kacie frowned. Mike had never mentioned anything.

"Oh, nothing scary, don't worry—but funny."

"Huh?"

"I can help you with your problem." Lucas gave her a wicked grin. "Hey! I *am* going to be a doctor one day, and that's what doctors do . . . right?"

This time, Kacie held her breath.

He touched her arm. "Stand still."

She stood there, melting in the heat that bounced off the sidewalk.

"Now tell me why you get words mixed up—why you don't say what you mean."

She whispered, "You knew that? Last night?"

"Of course, Weasel . . . well, I did after I thought about it."

"And it didn't upset you?"

"At first, yes, but this morning I saw things a different way, and it was fine."

"I guess I dwell on things too much."

"So think about it. What makes you mess up?"

She shrugged, and they walked again. "I speak up too fast . . . and then get scared I'll make mistakes."

"That's it, right there."

"What?"

"Fear."

"Yeah, right. Like it's easy for you to say. How can I stop fear? I don't even see it coming."

Lucas raised his arms. "Haven't you learned *anything* in church?"

"Sure I have, but if you mean faith . . . knowing it in here," she tapped her head, "and having it work are two different things."

"You're not messing up the words right now."

She stopped walking for a moment, then moved on slowly. "I . . . guess I couldn't make things any worse, so I stopped worrying."

"Yeah. And I bet faith's taken over. You know—faith casts out fear . . . ?"

Kacie brushed away a loose strand of hair. "I dunno . . . what if—"

"My dad always told me to pretend the other person's more afraid than you are. Works every time. Oh yeah—and you don't have to speak straight off. It's okay to take a second and think before answering."

"You mean it's happened to you?"

"When I was about fifteen, I never dared open my mouth."

She shot him a grin. "Who'd have ever thought?"

"Yeah, well, surprising what a few more years can do for a man."

Kacie sighed, wiping beads of sweat from her hairline. "And are you really still going to be a doctor?"

"What else? I was mad at you last night because my dad had just drilled me about his hopes for one of his sons taking over the family business. You hit a nerve, that's all."

"Your brothers might stay with your dad."

"That's what I'm thinking. Josh especially. He loves the work. Anyway, my mind's fixed. Whatever it takes, after my mission, I'm going to med school."

She punched him on the arm. "Good for you, Wolf . . . I mean, Lucas." Kacie blushed at his wide grin.

He leaned sideways and kissed her cheek. "Just practicing," he said.

Chapter 6

Santa's Helper on a Skateboard

(Clent, Worcestershire, England)

I wanted a mountain bike like snowflakes want cold weather. My friend, Max, got one for his fourteenth birthday last month. Cool blue and chrome with fifteen gears. He talked non-stop about riding through the Clent hills and forests a couple of miles from our village in the central part of England.

Christmas morning didn't produce the object I craved. Instead my gifts were a tracksuit, a new skateboard, and a job starting the day after tomorrow. A paper round. A six o'clock in the morning paper round!

How bad can things get?

Not only would I miss skimming over the hills, but I'd have to get up early, starting Wednesday. And it's holiday time. Staying-in-bed time.

What were my parents thinking? I can guess, of course. It's all about working for things you badly want, so you'll appreciate them. Old-fashioned baloney, if you ask me. Of course I'd appreciate that bike. Nothing could be more mind-blowing than flying along those mountain tracks. I'd be there every spare minute. Life was cruel at times.

It felt even crueler Wednesday morning.

"Come on, Dan," Mum whispered. "It's quarter to six. Rise and shine. There's porridge and hot black currant on the kitchen table."

I couldn't even focus properly. This must be a joke. It was liquorice black out there, freezing cold and lonely. The whole world was asleep, except for me—and my zany mother.

It was no joke, and breakfast didn't taste good. Lumpy porridge bounced in my stomach as I stumbled onto our porch. Muffled in tracksuit, red jacket, white scarf, red woolly hat, and boots, I felt like some undersized Santa.

"Now don't forget that houses fifty and sixty-six don't want papers delivered," Mum said, helping me stuff endless newspapers in the dirty yellow bags.

I lifted the sagging load onto my shoulder. "Mum, I don't want to sound weak or anything, but this is killing me. Have you felt the weight?"

"Never mind, dear. Think of the muscles you'll build. Here's your skateboard. And remember; be quiet in the block of flats. Elderly people don't like being wakened this early."

"Huh!" I muttered, heading lopsided down the path. "They're not the only ones."

The first morning was painful. I never realized how many different letterbox shapes there were. The wide ones move along with the newspaper. But others—I nearly lost my fingers a few times. Heavy gold ones that clamped down before the paper got right through were the worst. They looked posh, set in solid wooden doors, but their bite hurt.

I got a shock at one house. I slid a paper through the wide chrome flap in the front door, and heard a snarling thud as a body hit the other side. It snatched the paper, barely missing my fingers. My knees shook as I carried my skateboard down the path to the next house.

This time, a muffled figure was climbing into his car. He turned as he heard me coming.

"Ah, there you are, lad." The man actually sounded pleased to see me. No dogs. No fighting metal slits.

"I hoped you'd arrive before I left for work. We've been away, so we didn't give our usual tip this year. Here, have this." He put two pound coins into my hand in exchange for a paper. Two solid pounds!

"Thanks very much, sir." I stood, open-mouthed, wondering if I should shake his hand or something. But he was in the car and gone before I could move. I made mental notes never to take shortcuts over *that* man's garden.

I moved on. With feet half iced and fingers black with ink, I dreamed of earnings. If I got five pounds a week for sixteen weeks, in four months, even after tithing, there'd be enough for a secondhand bike. And I'd already earned two pounds. I pictured spring sunshine and scorching tires.

As six-thirty arrived, so did a lighter sky, and a few more people ventured out. Only ten houses to go.

I never even saw the small lad until I reached his doorstep, because something else caught my eye. The newspaper I was about to deliver fell open, and there, taking up a whole sheet of pictures, were bike adverts. Oh, how my feet itched for those pedals.

The sound of sniveling brought my head up sharp. It was too cold for anyone to sit outside, let alone a little tot in his pyjamas.

I whispered, trying not to frighten him. "Hey, what's up, mate?"

He lifted his brown curly head, then wiped a sleeve across his face. "Nothing."

I knew he lied. I mean, pyjamas aren't exactly outside gear, and that stone step wasn't the warmest place on earth.

I crouched at his level. "So why are you out here freezing?"

He squinted at me, as if weighing the friendship in my voice. Then he screwed up his face, pushing small fists at his eyes to hide the tears.

"Look, kid," I said, wondering how to get him inside without too much fuss. "It's Christmas week. Don't you want to go back in where it's warm and play with your toys?"

Wrong line. Sobs shook his body.

I dug in my coat pocket and handed him a dirty tissue, asking, "What's your name?"

His feet curled sideways on the cold stone. I took off my hat, wrapping it around his purple toes. He half smiled. I put my scarf around his shoulders.

"I'm Jamie," he said, "and . . . and . . . I wanted a bike for Christmas."

You too?

"But my . . . my dad left home before Christmas, and—"

"You mean you didn't get a bike after all?" I interrupted.

His big eyes looked up, reproaching me for being so dumb. "Yes, I did!"

"Sorry," I muttered. "Then why—?"

"I tried to tell you," he said. "My mum got one for me. She thinks I think it was Santa, but I know it wasn't 'cos I heard her talking on the phone. Anyway, all over Christmas I thinked and thinked. Dad always took me to get her present, but . . ." He scrubbed at fresh tears and hiccupped. "But this year no one did, and I didn't have anything for her."

He was shivering so much by now that I was worried. Suppose he got pneumonia or something, sat out here.

That's when the brain wave came.

I touched his arm. "Look, you go inside and stand by the window. I'll be back in fifteen minutes."

He rose to his feet, one finger stuck in his mouth, his face filled with awe. He nudged open the front door, and his voice was low and wondering, like something magical was beginning. "What you going to do?"

"You'll see," I called, skating away down the path.

By the time I'd finished the last delivery but one, I had second thoughts. Okay, so most of the shops were closed, except for Dillons. But . . . it would take all of two pounds to get a decent present there. The dream bike slid into the distance. I dragged it back. I needed every penny. The kid wouldn't really expect to see me again. It was a bizarre idea in the first place He'd be all right. He'd soon forget.

I battled my way toward the final letterbox—a gold one. As my cautious fingers dodged the gleaming flap, I suddenly pictured Jamie's pinched face gazing at me in owlish wonder. That did it. I slung the bag across my back and skated fast. Dillons looked warm, inviting.

The box of chocolates came to one pound eighty.

I raced back to Jaimie's house, my skateboard taking bumps in harmony with my legs and feet. A strange bubbling welled up inside—this time it wasn't the porridge.

Massive clouds began unloading snow, but I saw Jamie's window from several houses back, his nose flattened against the glass, face squashed and goggle-eyed.

By the time I'd reached Jamie's gate, jumped off the skateboard, and raced up the driveway, he was out on the doorstep, eyes and mouth all but meeting in one huge grin.

"You forgot these," he said, swapping my scarf and hat for the brightly wrapped box.

I caught his excitement. "What will you say to your mum?"

"Happy Christmas."

I nodded. "But where will you say the present came from?"

His reply was firm. "Santa's helper, of course."

I glanced down at my red jacket, feeling foolish. "Of course. Who else?"

The door closed, but curiosity got the better of me. Quietly lifting the letter flap, I peeped through. It was one of those scenes that locks in your mind forever.

Jamie yelled. "Mum, Mum!" She came rushing from the kitchen, then stopped in amazement, hands outstretched to receive her gift. Their faces shared a kind of glow, as if some magnetic power were zapping back and forth. I could almost touch the joy. My inside felt odd once more—happy odd—like something good melted and spread upward until it reached my throat.

The scene blurred. I let down the flap with a soft thunk and tiptoed back to the pavement where I left my board. I jumped on, dipping the back end and spinning.

The skateboard wasn't so bad after all.

Chapter 7

Joseph and His Technicolor Nightmare

(London, England)

This Christmas felt lame. I was fifteen years old, and I was playing Joseph in the Primary Nativity. I mean—at my age— parading with little kids in front of the whole Branch, dressed in an ancient dressing gown?

It was last Sunday when Sister Bailey, the Primary President, pulled me to one side before Priesthood. She looked so pleased to find me that her smile nearly reached her ears.

"Ah! Gabe," she began.

I recognized that tone. I knew what would follow. *You're precisely the—*

"You're precisely the person I've been looking for." She beamed. "We do miss you in Primary."

Her sparkling eyes gazed into mine. I felt her kindness getting to me the way it always did. I kept on walking as I spoke. "Hello, Sister Bailey. Thanks. I'm late for Priesthood."

She held my arm. "I won't keep you a minute, dear. I need your help. You don't mind, do you?"

"Um . . . no," I said, half nodding, half shaking my head.

She spoke faster. "You remember the old woolen dressing gown you wore as a shepherd in the Nativity one year? Would you mind wearing it again next week as Joseph? We don't have enough boys."

Her wide-eyed hope was too much. Besides, I was still catching my breath with relief that she didn't want me for an angel. So I agreed.

I must have been out of my mind. How was I going to live this one down? And that dressing gown itched something awful. Maybe if I pulled the headdress over my face, no one would know it was me.

I tried to forget the Nativity. It was the last week of school. For once, I was glad I was the only Church member there. As for my seminary teacher's suggestion that we share the Gospel as a Christmas gift, that's a no-brainer—not me, not at my school.

We finished school mid-week. Sunday came too fast. Our family planned to open gifts after church this year, as Christmas fell on Sunday. Strange how Mom and Dad never noticed I was the only one of their five children not groaning when that decision was made. My mind was on other things— other disastrous things.

My dad, who was the Branch President, and I arrived at church early. Straight into dress rehearsal.

I was reaching for a major itch at the top of my back when I first noticed someone crying. The sound came from behind a screen at the far end of the room. There was such a ruckus going on that no one else heard, and all I saw was a pair of small black feet in the gap at the bottom.

I inched the screen forward a bit. There she was. I guessed about four years old, with chubby, coffee colored cheeks, and two huge brown eyes dripping tears. I never saw her before, but then the Elders were always bringing investigators. New people were here all the time.

I whispered, holding out my hand, "Are you lost?"

She hiccupped. The tears slowed, but she didn't reply.

I tried a smile. "Look, I'm the one who should be crying, dressed in this wooly thing. Is your mum here?"

She nodded slowly, sticking her thumb in her mouth.

I knelt on the floor, hunching my back. "Climb on, and we'll find her."

Her smile was shaky. "The mishries brought me," she whispered. "They took Mam and Michael somewhere. I want to be an angel. I took off my shoes, but no one sees me." More tears welled.

I grinned, trying to sound cheerful, wishing I was the one hiding. "I expect that's because this big old screen's in the way."

I beckoned, flattening my back so she could reach. "What's your name?"

She giggled, small hands tugging at my costume, legs kicking and scrambling. Then she sniffed. "Leah."

She blew her nose on my head-cloth, and I shut my eyes, groaning inside. That was all I needed. I hoped the Young Women's choir didn't look too close when we walked in front of them.

I stood and tiptoed out of the Primary room, and was heading down the corridor when she gave a piercing yell, right in my ear. I nearly tripped. Another screech. "My Mam!" Leah jiggled up and down, tugging at the towel draped around my head.

I tried squinting past the cloth that now dangled over my eyes, and saw the group coming toward us. Leah slithered to the ground, dragging on my clothes to slow her progress. I pulled at my lopsided costume and looked again. A sick feeling surged in my throat.

I dropped the headpiece back over my face, but it was too late. He recognized me. Standing next to his mother, who scooped Leah into her arms, was Michael Mbuli—one of the lads from school.

My breath expelled on a long, silent, "Oh noooo!" If feelings made a person melt, I'd be a blob on the floor in seconds.

"Gabe?" Mike sounded incredulous. "Is that you, Gabe?" The grin that oozed across his face said everything.

Should I shrug it off with a laugh, pretending I often trailed through church looking like some ancient drifter? Or should I jabber in a foreign tongue and run off so he'd think he was mistaken?

I did neither because an odd thing happened. One thought made its way to the front of my mind—*be honest.*

I sighed, attempting a smile, and held out my hand. "Mike! I didn't realize you knew the Elders. I was bringing Leah to find her mum." My smile slipped. I turned to Mrs. Mbuli while pulling bits of clothing into shape, and mumbled. "I'm . . . uh . . . part of something we're putting on in the next meeting." Clearing my throat, I pointed toward Leah. "If you'd like to bring your daughter this way, I'm sure she can join the . . . um . . . show."

I didn't dare meet Mike's eyes. Imagination was bad enough. But on feeling his hand on my arm, I looked around—then stared in open-mouthed astonishment. How weird. He looked kind of interested.

"Don't suppose they'd have me too, would they, Gabe?" He sounded eager. "All this stuff the Elders have been teaching us about Jesus Christ. It's cool, man. And I thought you Mormons weren't Christian. Why have you never told me about your church?"

Before I could think of an excuse, he punched me on the shoulder, and taking Leah from his mother, marched off down the corridor.

With a half wave at Mrs. Mbuli and the grinning Elders, I walked to the Primary Room.

This couldn't be happening. Mike, of all people. He was the class clown, famous for saying what he thought. Mike? In the Nativity?

And he was. Sister Bailey jumped at the chance of an extra Wise Man—especially a tall, dark, handsome one. And no one in the congregation minded when one small, bare-footed angel crept up to hold his hand.

But the bit that got to me was when we sang *Picture a Stable.* It was new to Mike, so he stood there silent and dignified. I watched, and chills ran down my back as tears rolled down his cheeks.

Something was happening between him and the Lord. I felt it.

Chapter 8

You'll Never Get a Banana Tree

(Bridgestone, Connecticut, USA)

I didn't see the point of sticking to rules.

Dad was a dentist, and Mom was always busy with my younger brother and sister, and with her social life. No one had time to check on me, so I did what I wanted. Dad had scads of money, and I was sure he'd bail me out if anything ever went wrong.

My name wasn't King for nothing. Marcus King, age sixteen, and tall for my age. But the gang called me King because I got the best ideas, and because my Roman nose looked regal. Got that word "regal" from a British kid who came to our school in Bridgestone, Connecticut on an exchange student visit from England. He said regal meant royal.

"You look like King George the Fourth," he told me. "It's your big nose and the way your bottom lip sticks out under your top lip—and those fierce eyebrows."

I'd never heard of the guy, so it didn't mean much. But it sure built my reputation at school. I was a leader. Kids followed me.

Nate and Brian *always* followed me. Last Friday we headed for a party at Jody's house. Her parents were away for the weekend, so she invited a bunch of us from school. I picked up Nate and Brian and sped down the street, my headlights carving through the slanting November sleet.

Nate punched the headrest behind me, making my head bounce as he shouted through the braces on his front teeth, "School sucks rocks!"

"Quit hitting!" I yelled, taking one hand off the wheel to rub my sore neck. I felt Nate's long legs kneeing my back through the leather seat.

Brian sat in front with me. He twisted around, stretching out an arm like he meant to hit Nate, but clipped my highlighted spikes instead. I ducked, growling at them. "Quit messing around, or you can both walk."

Nate yanked on Brian's mop of black hair, his voice loud in my ear. "I'm not joking. I'm done, finished. That Mrs. Chase failed me one time too many." He opened the window, yelling into the wind and rain, "School sucks rocks."

I laughed. "You made that old lady at the bus stop jump. She wasn't expecting that."

Nate closed the window and slumped, grumbling. "Yeah, well . . . I wasn't expecting to fail history again, either."

I caught a glimpse of him in the rear-view mirror, illuminated by the street lights as we drove by. His thin lips compressed over his braces, and his long face creased in a mean frown. Nate is trouble when he looks that way. Not that I've got anything against trouble, but I haven't been driving long. I wasn't sure I could deal with his tantrum and steer at the same time.

Brian whooped and pressed the window control, letting in another blast of cold air. I glanced across as he opened his full-lipped mouth wide, slurping in the wet wind.

"Faster, King," he yelled. "See that girl pushing a bike? I want her number." He gave a high-pitched laugh and stuck out his head. "Watch it, lady! There's a maniac loose, and he's coming your way!"

I put my foot to the floor, and we jolted forward, howling with laughter. I drove with one hand, using the other to wipe my eyes so I could see the road.

Out in the pouring rain, a young boy appeared from nowhere, crossing right in front of us. I slammed on the brakes, skidding and spinning until we hit something solid. The engine stalled.

There was a long silence. Then Nate and Brian starting yelling.

"What's going on?"

"Where's the kid?"

"Did we hit him?"

"Let me out!"

I peered through the steamed-up window, breathing fast. If I'd believed in God, I would have prayed. Then I let out a whistle of relief. The boy was sprinting away from us down the road. I tried the door, but it wouldn't open. Looking ahead, I saw a low wall glinting in the headlight beam. My laugh was shaky. "It's only a wall, guys. We hit a stupid wall."

Brian wriggled his shoulders and stretched his legs. His voice sounded more confident than he looked. "Whoa! Nice one, King. Hope there's no cops around."

I just sat there, totally creeped out. A joke's a joke. But hey, the thought of killing a kid freaked me. I forced a laugh. "Give me a break." I spoke loud to hide the nerves. "I can sniff cops a mile away. Let's get to that party."

After a couple of tries, the engine roared, and we all relaxed. I drove the rest of the way with both hands on the wheel, concentrating more than usual.

The basement party was packed by the time we arrived. That's the way I like parties—girls and music going full blast. People stared as we sauntered in. I wore jeans and a black shirt. Nate and Brian both wore jeans and blue T-shirts.

"Let's get this party started," I said to Brian and Nate, leading the way. "Which girls can we make interested in us instead of the guys they came with?" I expanded my chest and walked tall. "Better hurry, guys, or I'll get 'em all."

Brian sneered. "Yeah, like last time? When Jenny Charles slapped your face?"

I grinned. "At least her date didn't."

"Duh," Nate said. "He's a Mormon. Jed Finch wouldn't swat a fly, let alone your sinful face."

We proceeded with my plan. Jody Parson's home was huge, and the barely-lit dance area ran through most of the basement.

So there was plenty of room to hit and run. After a couple of victories, I noticed a ruckus in the far corner by the stairs. People gathered around a couple of kids, elbowing each other, eyes wide, excited.

Nate, Brian, and I squeezed past sweating bodies. I nudged Nate, leaning close so he could hear me shout above the music. "What's in the bottles?"

Nate yelled, "Dunno. Not soda."

"Whisky," Brian called. He was near the front by now. "Jason's brought whisky."

It didn't take long for at least half the party to stop dancing and join us by the stairs. I glanced around, not wanting to be left out, but still smarting from the near miss with the kid on the bike.

Brian poked my arm. "Go on, King. We'll follow you."

I joked, "You first."

"What's wrong with you?"

"Nothing," I lied.

Brian interrupted. "Hey guys, look over there." He pointed at a group behind Jason and the whiskey. In the middle stood Jed Finch, the Mormon. Five guys were shoving and bumping Finch, swearing in his face.

Brian yelled over the heads in front. "Go on, geek. Once won't hurt. Show us what you're really made of."

Nate joined in. "Yeah," he cried. "We won't tell."

I watched, amused, wondering what Finch would do, willing him on, but at the same time half hoping he wouldn't give way. When they pushed him against the stairs, he fell backward onto the second step.

Then Jed Finch rose to his feet, still on the step. The room went a bit quieter. He looked kind of majestic standing there above us all—his short, clay-colored hair neat, brown eyes sharp, and his mouth a tight line. When he spoke, it was strong—not loud, not angry—but real strong.

"Sorry, guys, you'll have to count me out." He raised his hand, a quick smile cracking his lips. "I'd rather stay in control. See you Monday."

He straightened his light-blue shirt and walked up the stairs, not once looking at the rest of us who mumbled and shuffled, waiting for someone to speak.

I filled the silence like I always do—with smart words that get a laugh. "That's the last time he's invited."

"Right," Brian said. "Okay, King, no more stalling. You're turn for the bottle."

"Do you want me to drive, or don't you?"

"Give him a break, Brian," Nate said. "We need him to drive. I'm too young to die."

* * *

I remembered Nate's words the following week, and wished he'd never spoken them—as if taking them back could, in some way, put right what happened on Wednesday.

As soon as I walked through the door after school, I knew something was wrong. Nine-year-old Hannah, and Adam, twelve, sat at the kitchen table looking scared. Mom was on the phone, her voice edgy, like she was struggling to hold it together. "Yes, Officer. I'll be there right away. Yes. I . . . I'll bring his things."

"What's up, Mom," I said, not liking the feeling in my stomach.

Her hands shook. "It's your dad." She bit her bottom lip to stop it from wobbling. "Oh, this is terrible. There's been an accident. Dad's in the hospital—one leg broken, and his right hand is smashed." Her voice broke. "The kid driving the other car was drunk. He's dead."

She sank onto the nearest chair, and I went to her, putting my arm around her shoulder, my own hands trembling. A tight lump burned my throat. *How could this happen? Not to our family. Things like this only happened to other people.*

Mom left for the hospital, leaving me in charge of Hannah and Adam. She hadn't come home by the time I got them in bed, so I waited up to make sure she was okay. She wasn't. She came home at midnight and cried and drank tea for another half hour before I talked her into getting some sleep.

I went to my room and undressed, feeling like some robot in Star Wars. But lying down brought on more thinking. *How will Dad keep working? And if he can't, who will pay to look after us all? And worse—what about my car? Will I still have one?* This last thought had me tossing for a long time. Life without a car was unthinkable. It was nearly three o'clock in the morning before I slept—and then not deep. I woke up every time the dreams came—dreams of driving drunk, hitting that kid, who turned into Dad, who wouldn't get up and walk.

The next evening we visited Dad. Mom was already there, so we all gathered around the hospital bed. It had been a tough day. I hadn't gone to school. Wasn't sure I could cope. But being at home with all the family drama was worse.

Dad spoke to Mom in a broken voice. "How am I supposed to keep working in dentistry? That's what I want to know." He rubbed his bald head with his good hand. "I could manage with a useless foot, but my hand . . .?" His face twisted with pain. "The doctor says it'll never return to normal."

Mom brushed away some tears. "I don't know why this is happening. It's all so unfair. All those years of working so hard, building up the business—destroyed in a split second. Why did God let this happen to us?" Her voice rose to a thin, high sound. "And it's Christmas next month."

I just sat there, not speaking. I couldn't stand much more of this. I'd been feeding these same kinds of thoughts into my brain since yesterday. It wasn't only Dad and the business. Our whole family was affected. Hannah and Adam looked as if they'd never smile again, Mom spouted tears like sprinklers programmed for drought.

And Dad? He wasn't like Dad at all anymore—lying in that hospital bed with his confidence all gone.

For some strange reason, this last thought made me remember Jed Finch standing on that stair at the party, looking as regal as a Jedi Master. The image was vivid and hard to push away. *That guy's so not cool.* But I had to admit, he had some sort of extra nerve that didn't upset easily. Not like my family, all caving in.

We fell apart on the way home. We fell apart every day until

Dad came out of hospital—and then we fell apart some more.

Take the TV, for instance. Adam whined to Mom, "I'm sick of old movies. Why does Dad have to watch them all the time? When's it our turn?"

Mom shook her head. She had a hard time not shouting—I knew from the way her jaw went stiff, and the words squeezed out through her teeth. "Go outside and play, Adam."

Wednesday night I'd gone to my bedroom at nine, and crashed on my bed to avoid my miserable family. The grey drapes were open, so I lay there, staring at blackness, my mind pitching bits of Mom and Dad's endless discussions back and forth. They'd been taking it out on God again.

"What have we done to deserve this?" Mom had said, tucking a red fleece blanket around Dad's legs as he watched John Wayne in *The Big Trail* for the fifth time.

"Don't know," he muttered, moving his head to see the screen Mom blocked. "But one thing's for sure—I'm not God's favorite person."

"I'm not sure I even believe in God any more." Mom fixed the cushion behind Dad's head. "I mean, why should this happen to you, of all people? Why didn't God stop such a dreadful thing?"

Now, I wasn't all that convinced about God, either. I guess I almost believed he was out there, somewhere, but I never needed him.

Until now.

This last thought made me shoot upright.

Me? The independent King? Needing God? Oh sure.

I swung my legs onto the floor, dropping my head into my hands. I didn't need help from anyone, let alone a vague person who may or may not be out there in space.

But what about the family? I flipped onto the bedcovers and tried to block out this new thought . . . but it kept on coming. Okay, so maybe I could get by on my own. But what about Mom and Dad? They could sure use help right now. The way things were going, family life would soon be out of control.

Control. There it was again. That image of Jed Finch. Controlled, steady. I eventually drifted off to sleep, still in my

Levis and my old blue shirt. But Finch wouldn't leave, not even in my dreams. He kept offering to help me. Something to do with Dad, but I couldn't hang onto the dream long enough to follow it through. By the time morning came, I had this strong gut feeling that I should do something that went totally against anything I've ever done before.

I waited all day for just the right moment—one minute chickening out, the next minute prepared to look an idiot. By the time school ended, the thing was building up inside ready to burst. I had to speak to Finch, and I couldn't let anyone else hear—especially not Brian and Nate.

I grabbed the pair of them as soon as class finished, at the same time keeping an eye on Finch, who was packing his bag, ready to leave.

"I'll catch up with you later," I said to Nate. "I want to see Mrs. Chase about tonight's assignment."

He grimaced. "Watch out. She'll jump all over you if you get it wrong."

I punched him on the arm. "That's why I'm asking, dude. I don't need another failure."

Brian pulled him away. "Move it, Nate. I want to buy donuts before the bus leaves."

Only a few students were left in the room. Jed Finch was still at his desk, messing with something in his bag. I didn't dare speak to Mrs. Chase, in case I missed Finch. In the end, I walked toward him and stood there, staring.

He looked up, his face wary.

I kept my voice low. "We have to talk." I glanced at the teacher and turned my face sideways, whispering, "Meet me outside the baseball changing rooms in ten minutes."

Mrs. Chase left the room, letting the door slam behind her.

Finch gazed at me as though I'd lost it. "What for?"

"Relax, man. It's nothing bad. Honest."

"If it's not bad, then tell me here."

"Come on, Finch." My face reddened. *What I say goes, or there are consequences. Everyone knows that. Why doesn't this punk understand?* I couldn't let him make a fool of me, but I was too far in. I tried again, disgusted at having to beg, but for some reason unable to stop.

"I only want to ask something. Don't make me crawl or—"

"Or what? If that's a threat, I'm not taking it."

I swung around and stomped out of the room. *I knew this was a mistake. Why did I ever try in the first place?* By then I'd missed talking to Mrs. Chase *and* missed the bus. I made for home, head down, furious with myself for looking stupid.

I'd reached the gas station when I heard running footsteps behind me. I swung around thinking it was Brian or Nate. I was in no mood for conversation. But it was Jed Finch.

I looked away. "You're too late. I changed my mind." Before he could respond, I went on, "It's no good talking here. Too many people." I did a quick check up and down the street. Not a soul in sight. I shrugged it off. "Okay, so people might come."

Finch shook his head, sighing. "Do you need something, or not?"

I bit back a smart remark because a now-or-never feeling filled my head. I moved closer. "It's like this . . . I know you're not going to believe me, but . . . I really do need your help."

I told him the whole story about Dad's accident and our despairing family. I left out the weird dreams.

"You've got to come," I begged, out of breath and out of pride, the whole situation weighing on me like some wild storm cloud. "I've watched you. You have something. If you could talk to my dad . . . he needs something right now. Anyway . . ." I looked down at the sidewalk where a big crack split the concrete into two levels. "Anyway, I have no idea what you can do for us, so I guess it was a brainless plan after all."

He stood there in silence, looking at his feet.

I turned to go, feeling more like an idiot than ever, convinced I must have gone completely nuts. I punched the air and let out a groan.

"No," Finch said, catching hold of my arm. "I mean . . . don't leave. I'll come. Just surprised, that's all." He grinned. "But I'll help if I can. When—?"

"They're home right now."

His eyebrows shot up, and he coughed. "Uh . . . why not? Now's fine with me . . . I guess."

We'd got this far, and there was no escape. I couldn't think what to talk about while trudging along the sidewalk next to Finch. He was a few inches shorter than me, and until then, tall always meant smarter. But looking down at him no longer seemed to make a difference.

We rounded a bend in the road, and the sea at Lighthouse Point flickered in the distance. The rain started, and we hunched into our jackets. Mine was navy, fleece-lined. Finch's had worn out cuffs, no fleece. It might have been green once, but looked almost black.

Jed Finch seemed nervous as we neared our house.

"You're not going to let me down?" I said.

He pulled at the collar of his grey sweater under the jacket, stretching his neck. "Nope. I can hardly wait."

We reached the porch, and I cracked open the door, glancing down the hall into the front room. Dad was on the recliner, reading a paper, holding it with his one good hand. And judging from the sound of gunshot, Hannah and Adam had finally got their way and were watching TV.

Dad looked up as I pushed Finch forward.

Before I could change my mind, I blurted out, "Thought you'd like to meet a friend. His name's Jed Finch."

Dad's long face looked more pinched than normal. One plastered arm lay on top of the blanket, and the fiberglass cast on his leg poked out the bottom end. He grunted. "Sorry, I can't shake hands. I expect Marcus told you . . ." He glared at me. "Have I met this young man before?"

"Dad . . . I . . ."

The plan wasn't working. I knew Dad's look meant he didn't want strangers hanging around right now. I scratched my head and glanced away. "Where's Mom?"

"Upstairs. Been to the store."

I reached the bottom stair the same moment Mom appeared at the top. My mouth dried up. This was never going to work. What was I doing? I had no clue where or how to begin.

Jed Finch cleared his throat and took over. "Mr. and Mrs. King?" He paused. "May I sit?"

Dad indicated the couch, and I followed Mom to the loveseat. I sat there, cracking my fingers, wondering what was coming. By that time, Adam and Hannah had switched off the TV and sat next to each other on the floor by Dad's feet, eyeing Finch and me with wide-eyed curiosity.

Finch leaned forward, his hands clasped, arms resting on his knees. His head came up, and he smiled, first at Dad, and then at the rest of us in turn. I could have sworn he was enjoying this. Wish I could say the same for me.

Finch's voice was warm and easy. "Yes, Mr. King, Marcus told me, and I'm very sorry. It must be the worst kind of situation you're facing."

"I don't want to bore you, young man," Dad said, "but if you had hours to listen to this disaster, it wouldn't be long enough."

"I think the reason King . . . I mean, Marcus . . . asked me to visit, is because of my belief in God."

"Ah, now wait a minute." Dad sat upright, letting the newspaper slide to the floor. "No time for God in this family. Where was he in all this? Why would God—if he's there—let such a dreadful thing happen? Answer me that."

"Oh, he's there all right . . . Sir. But he's given us a unique gift. It's a law called free agency. Everyone has it—even the drunk kid who lost his life and caused all this grief."

Dad dipped his head, tucking in his double chin. He and Mom frowned at each other.

Finch went on. "It means God can't step in and prevent every disaster, because that goes against the laws of nature. Freedom to choose allows people to feel the consequence of sin. Otherwise no one would ever change or move forward."

Everyone was silent. Dad's eyes narrowed. "What do you mean? I don't see the connection with our situation."

"If you plant a tomato," Finch said, "you'll never get a banana tree."

Hannah, who sat cross-legged, chin cupped in hands, giggled for the first time since the accident. Her blonde curls bobbed up and down. "I get it. I get it." She twisted around, beaming at Dad. "We can choose what we do, but we can't choose what happens after, 'cus tomatoes don't grow into bananas."

Adam shook his head and shoved his sister. "She's getting mixed up. She means God couldn't stop the drunk kid, because God has to stick to rules. Like if I hit Hannah, God can't jump in and stop her getting hurt." He grinned.

Hannah squealed. "That's what I said!"

Finch nodded and looked at Dad. "Mr. King," he said—and his next words blew me away. "I'd like to suggest the rest of us kneel around your chair, and we have a prayer together." He rushed on before Dad could get a word in. "You see, I believe that in this life we are meant to have problems, and we grow by living through them . . . if we turn to God. Asking him for help lets him to put things right in his own way, which we can't always do by ourselves."

Finch raised his eyebrows at Mom, a smile hovering on his lips. "I don't mind offering the prayer . . . if you all agree, that is."

Both Mom and Dad looked like their minds were ripping open. I swallowed, wondering how they could refuse. This guy certainly had something. He was either crazy, or he knew what he was talking about. Either way, I felt the tension mounting.

Finch didn't wait. He knelt, beckoning the rest of us to follow. "Thank you. It's really the best I can do right now."

After we got to the floor, there was an embarrassed hush.

Finch prayed with quiet, simple, and direct words. He asked for a spirit of light to be upon our family, a light that would bring peace, forgiveness, healing, and direction for us all. Then he stood and went round the circle shaking hands.

Tears welled in Mom's eyes, and I noticed the stress lines on Dad's forehead relaxing. Something felt different. Couldn't say what, exactly, but it was definitely there—like a shadow rising.

I accompanied Finch to the door and followed him outside. "Thanks . . . uh . . . Jed. You were good in there."

I wondered again at the guy's coolness. I could never have done what he did, never in a thousand light-years.

Jed smiled.

"Um . . . there's one more thing," I said, kicking at a loose stone on the driveway.

"Sure. No problem."

"Don't tell anyone at school about this, okay?"

Jed Finch looked at me a few seconds before replying. "If that's what you want, it's fine with me." He gave me a crooked grin, and his eyes softened in an odd way, like he was going to say something and then changed his mind. He turned and walked away.

I dug my hands in my Levi pockets and stood there, watching him go. Yep! That guy Finch was strange, all right.

But that's okay. I can handle strange.

Chapter 9

Darkness at Noonday

(Elmer, New Jersey, USA)

"Life's not fair!" Bryce Norton twisted her long auburn hair around her fingers.

Asher, who'd been around since she was Primary age, raised his eyebrows. They were the last youth in the foyer waiting for a ride home from seminary.

Bryce turned to the notice board, jabbing a finger at a dazzling poster. "New Year's Social, it says." She jabbed again. "Bring a date, it says. How can I? There's no one to ask me."

She slumped onto the bench, picturing a dateless Christmas, dateless New Year, dateless forever.

Asher pulled himself straight. He was short and skinny, and had a cheerful face sprinkled with freckles. "So, Mike, Seth, and I are no one, are we? I'll remember that next time you want your bike fixed, or—"

"Okay, okay, I'm sorry. But you've always been here. You're like . . . well . . . brothers. Dating's different."

"Yeah, right."

"A date should be exciting." She tossed her head, putting on a dramatic voice. "I want to be whirled off my feet by someone tender on the inside, but tough on the outside. Someone hard to reach, but cool and—"

"Mushy."

"Excuse me?"

"Keep it real. If you're expecting some rich dude to roll up in a limo, it's not going to happen." He picked up his scriptures. "There's your mom's Honda. Scoot! She's backing up already."

Bryce reached for her backpack and handed Asher a seminary booklet that lay next to hers on the bench. She buttoned her green jacket, then paused. "Asher?"

He tugged at the heavy door. "We have to go."

She kept talking. "Between you and me, am I'm pretty enough to get a date?"

Asher gave an exasperated sigh and looked away. "Yeah."

"Then why don't I?"

He stood quiet, keeping the door open with his foot. Then he grinned and waved the booklet at her. "Read D and C section ninety-five, verse six."

Bryce poked him in the ribs and brushed past, head in the air. "Oh, you're so . . . so . . . serious." She ran, calling over her shoulder. "Move it then. Last one to the car buys drinks on the way home."

Asher took a shortcut, hedge-hopping a stone wall and a few lifeless rose bushes. Bryce came in a close second. He bent over, panting, then smiled. "The drink's on me, anyway."

"Thanks." She gasped, regaining her breath as he opened the car door.

Her mother revved the engine, and Asher's smile widened. "And some for Sister Norton, since we made her wait."

Before the dome light switched off, Bryce caught a warm expression in Asher's brown eyes. She felt kindness coming right at her. How had she never seen his eyes do that before?

* * *

The following weekend brought snow and ice—a typical New Jersey winter day. The atmosphere in Sunday School wasn't much warmer, because earlier that morning Bryce had read Doctrine and Covenants section ninety-five, verse six. *They who are not chosen have sinned a very grievous sin, in that they are walking in darkness at noonday.*

How could Asher say that? A sin? Come on—it wasn't her fault she wasn't chosen. She'd sniffed away tears and brushed her hair extra hard.

Now she sat in class ready for battle.

"What's up, Bryce?" Asher dropped into the empty chair on her left. "You look like you're having a good-cheer famine."

She glared at him. "You're so . . . not smart."

Asher frowned, pulling back.

"You really took that verse six out of context."

He cringed, giving a sheepish grin. "Oh . . . that."

Bryce turned away, chin up. "Why is it a sin to have no date? And I'm not in darkness." Her voice rose a notch, wobbling. "Everything's bright and sunny, thank you."

Asher burst out laughing. He touched her arm. "Hey, you're not . . . I mean . . . uh-oh. It was a kind of joke. You know—playing with words."

Bryce bent her head, letting long strands of hair hide her face. Her voice was small. "It wasn't funny."

"You seriously don't think—"

At that moment, the teacher walked in the door, and Asher stopped talking.

* * *

By the time midweek seminary came around again, Bryce had melted a little and saw the funny side. Walking in darkness? Who did Asher think she'd missed around here? She giggled. It was worth catching the early bus to seminary and getting there in time for some teasing.

But Asher didn't show. No one had heard from him all week. Strange. Asher never missed seminary.

Bryce forgot all about Asher when Mom arrived at nine.

Mom spoke as soon as Bryce opened the car door. "You'll never believe what happened. Thought I was seeing things. But they were real all right. I think. No time to double-check. But I mean . . . bananas? At this time of year?"

"Mom, what are you saying?"

"They were there, honey. On a tree in the front yard. Bunches of bananas all over the branches."

"Come on, Mom. Bananas don't grow in New Jersey. You're imagining things."

Mom switched on the engine. "I may confuse easily, but I'm not senile."

The home journey went faster than usual. And sure enough, there in the front yard was a banana tree.

Bryce zipped her fleece jacket and clambered out in a daze, half aware of a telephone ringing in the distance. She wandered toward the tree, reaching for the nearest banana, calling over her shoulder. "Must be a joke, Mom. They're tied on."

But Mom was already at the house. "I'll get the phone."

Bryce shivered and tugged at the fruit. It felt cold and slimy where the skin had been peeled, then stuck back together with tape. Her eyes stretched wide. Folded in a neat square under the surface was a piece of paper. With chilled fingers, she managed to straighten the paper enough to read.

Is this an exciting, romantic, and different enough way to ask for a date? If so, please climb the nearest branch and pull down banana number two—the one with a red heart on top.

Bryce took a deep breath, hands on hips. Asher! She clambered up the lumpy trunk onto the first branch and found the next banana. The heart had slipped, but another message opened up inside it.

Well, you've been whisked off your feet, and this fruit is tender on the inside and tough on the outside.

"Is he kidding?" she muttered, prodding the banana, now squishy and turning brown.

She read on. *Now go for the fruit on that branch overhanging the hedge—the one with two hearts. Be careful. It's not easy.*

Bryce hesitated, then scrambled and slithered until she was stretched across the hedge top. But she couldn't hold on and slid face-down into scratchy branches. She spat frosted twigs from her mouth, and reached again, grabbing at the banana. Brown pulp squirted in her hands, and she squealed. "Oh, Asher Harper! Wait 'til I get you!"

She dropped the banana and jumped down, bending to brush sticky fingers across the icy grass. Then she straightened. Might as well take a peek at the note, seeing as now she'd got this far. She picked out the last piece of paper and read out loud. *So sorry this one was hard to reach, but it's definitely cool and—"*

"Mushy?" came a familiar voice from behind the hedge.

Bryce exploded. "Exactly!" She tossed her hair, then pulled down another banana. In seconds war broke out, and the air rang with shrieks and Asher's infectious laughter.

When all the bananas were off the tree, Bryce stood still, hands on hips. "So this is where you were during seminary. You're totally whacko. What can I say?" She shook her head, brushing bits of tree off her jacket.

He pulled a roll of paper towels from under the hedge, tore off a sheet, and gently wiped banana mush from her hands. His voice was soft. "You could answer my question."

"Which one?"

"Will you be my date for the New Year's social?"

She looked at him—standing there in his dark blue jacket and navy knitted hat. There was that smile again, floating in his eyes, only this time it was anxious and hopeful. She looked away. Maybe it didn't matter that he'd been around forever. He cared, despite knowing her so well. Perhaps she should check out the real Asher.

"I must be crazy, but . . . yes. On two conditions."

Asher knelt in the slush at her feet, his voice deep and solemn. "Whatever." Then, with a grand gesture, he pulled out a box of chocolates from inside his jacket. "And here's a cool surprise to make up for the not-so-cool surprise."

Bryce giggled.

He placed the chocolates in her outstretched hand.

She tucked the box under one arm and pulled him to his feet. "Okay, I'll be your date, but only if there are no more bananas."

"And the other condition?"

She paused. "Does this mean I stop walking in darkness at noonday?"

Asher grinned. "It's never dark with me around. Come on, let's party."

"Is Mom's hot apple and lemon with cinnamon toast party enough?"

Asher closed his eye, breathing in and letting out a long "Ahhhh!"

Bryce nudged him toward the house. The mess could wait a few hours. Dates don't grow on trees.

Chapter 10

Mountain Nearing

(Manchester, England)

We all did it—all except for Jordan, that is. It seemed the cool thing. I mean, it felt good—seeing the funny side, being quick and clever with words.

Jordan thought I went too far.

"Aaron Veasey, you're such a hypocrite," she said to me this morning at school. "How can you sit in church on Sunday, giving all the right answers, then act like a sarcastic creep today?"

Most of the time I liked Jordan. She'd been around for twelve of my fourteen years, and was small and fiery, with big eyes the color of stormy skies. Her desk stood in front of mine.

I flicked her ponytail around with my ruler. "I don't see the connection. Church stuff and school stuff? They're different."

She had a way of wrinkling her nose when she disagreed, and she wrinkled it right then. She looked kind of pretty when she did that. But she wasn't telling *me* what to do.

"I'll tell you the connection," she said. "It *hurts*. That's what."

"Making people laugh hurts?"

"What about the one being laughed at? Just because you don't see hurt, doesn't mean it's not there." She sniffed.

Now when Jordan sniffed like that, it meant she'd found a cause. She called them her mountains, because a Sunday school teacher once quoted Caleb in the Old Testament where he says,

"Give me this mountain." She'd watched for them ever since. And that was okay with me, as long as she was the one doing the climbing. But as soon as she hooked into *my* comfort zone . . . no deal!

"What about that little kid on the bus this morning?" I said. "He was laughing with the rest of us."

"At first." She shook her head. "You didn't see his eyes tear up when he realized you made him look stupid."

"Well he *was* stupid—saying his name was Walk."

"It was logical. He said people call a fly a Fly because it flies. Therefore today he wants to be called Walk because he walks. Makes sense to a five year old." She sniffed again, nose in the air. "You didn't need to add, 'You should be called Dumbo because you're dumb.'"

Before I could have the last word, in came our geography teacher. But it was a waste of time hoping Jordan would forget her cause.

"I suppose you're sitting there dreaming up more sarcasm," she threw at me next day, first lesson.

I jumped. I couldn't admit I'd been gazing out at the misty morning, looking at a spider's web strung between two posts. The rain and wind played with the strands, ballooning and sucking them in all directions. But the spider had worked hard, and the wind couldn't undo that work.

"Of course." I grinned, straightening in my chair. "And if you weren't so tough, I'd throw some your way."

She laughed. "Wouldn't do you much good." She set her backpack on the floor. "I'm getting expert at forgiving."

"Wahoo for you, Miss Perfect. Want a halo?" I was about to add, "Let me know if it slips, and I'll send for mountain rescue," but Registration began, so I just poked her in the back instead.

During the announcements, Miss Gale, our class teacher, produced a letter. "We've been given a different assignment for our winter service project this year." She smiled. "There's a special school close to Manchester. The children are spastic and range in age from five to eighteen. They'd like as many volunteers as possible—one young man and woman to a pair—for an hour after school, once a week. So I'm sending round a sign-up sheet."

I groaned, switching off while she read more details. I was scared of handicapped people. I liked to feel comfortable, on the same wavelength as those around me. That wasn't difficult when you were on the same level—but what level were *they* on?

Besides, it meant missing my favorite TV show.

Jordan joined me at the bus stop after school. "Have you signed up for the service project then, Aaron?" She gave me a sweet smile, head to one side.

"Oh sure! I've booked for each day of the week." I glared down at her. "*Not!*"

She shrugged. "Suit yourself."

"Those people are on a different planet," I said. "You won't catch me pushing wheelchairs and wiping noses."

"How about you do the pushing, and me the wiping?" Her smile grew wider. With her eyebrows raised like that, she could charm the plaque off your teeth.

But she wouldn't get me this time. I firmed up my voice. "By the time we've traveled there and back, and spent an hour at the school, *Lost* will have ended on TV. Besides, I'll be starving. Then homework on top of all that? You've got to be joking."

"You know what?" She glanced quickly at me, then down at the toe of her shoe tracing circles in the mud. "I was going to suggest my mum tapes *Lost*, and I make some of those thick chocolate brownies to eat on the bus." She moved away. "Don't worry. I'll find someone else . . . chocolate cake, too, would be—"

"Wait!" I grasped her arm. "I didn't exactly say no, did I?" Jordan Grundy's mum makes *the* most mouth-watering brownies. "I'll . . . think about it. Maybe it won't be so bad. A week's trial might work."

* * *

I spent seven bad days wishing I'd never agreed to tackle this particular mountain of Jordan's. If it hadn't been for the brownie craving, I might still have backed out.

Friday crawled nearer.

It finally came, and we walked to the main bus stop. Jordan saved half the brownies for the return journey. How did she guess I might eat and run? When I saw all those youngsters in wheelchairs, I very nearly *did* run—forget the brownies.

An older looking nurse with crinkled gray hair and a fixed smile introduced Jordan and me to a blond-haired boy. "This is Luke. He's fourteen." She handed us a pack of paper towels. "He's a permanent resident and loves to draw." The nurse marched on, matching more patients with students.

I gulped. *Draw?*

Luke's arms and legs were thrashing all over. How could he keep still long enough to draw? And it wasn't his nose that needed wiping—it was his mouth. Dribbles dropped down his chin and neck.

I looked away.

"Here." Jordan leaned forward, gently mopping up the mess. "Take it easy, Luke. We won't disappear." She smiled at him, making eye contact, leaning close. "I'm Jordan, and this is Aaron. Talk slowly. What would you like us to do?"

Luke—one of his big blue eyes drooping and twitching—spoke awkwardly. "Thanks. I'm not embarrassed, if you're not." His smile was lopsided. "Come on. Let's draw."

My jaw dropped.

Luke wheeled his chair at high speed toward the table in the middle of the room . . . and missed. He shot past, laughing and waving. I ran, grabbed the handles, and spun him around so fast he nearly toppled out.

He shouted, slurring the words with excitement. "That was great. Let's do it again!"

By then I was laughing, too. "Um . . . let's not. Here, get this pencil between your fingers."

With me holding one of his arms, and Jordan restraining the other so his hand could still move, Luke guided that pencil over the paper.

He was almost on our level in an odd sort of way.

Now, next to being the Master of Sarcasm—and therefore brilliant with words—art was my favorite subject. Words and art went together. Some of those old poets—like Wordsworth—knew what they were doing when they lived in wild and scenic places. I watched Luke outline trees, flowers, mountains, and meadows with sweeping strokes, and knew I was seeing something unreal.

Jordan looked awestruck, too. "How do you know all this, Luke?"

He gave another shaky grin—and more dribbles. The words came slowly. "Books. TV. Videos. One day, I'll find all this . . . this p . . . paradise." He tugged the pencil upward. "Know what? Trees and flowers are like me. Solid inside. No control outside. I know how it feels." He aimed the pencil at his chest. "They hurt in here when someone's mean."

With each passing week I knew I couldn't stop visiting Luke. I got used to the dribbles, though I always let Jordan use the Kleenex tissue. The odd thing was I could never bring myself to be sarcastic in front of him. Perhaps it was the strange way he had of pure thinking. It was like this boy's body got windblown in all directions, ballooning out where it wasn't expected. Yet his mind stayed in place, holding onto life and making it shine. He was anchored on the inside.

And pretty soon when others at school told spastic jokes, it made me clench my fists. I wanted to strike out and protect someone, even though there was no one around who needed protecting.

Then one visit, I forgot I wasn't with school friends. Luke had been ill. He was on tablets for almost everything. Chest infections hit him worse than most of us.

Cicely, the gray-haired nurse, showed us to his room with her usual wide smile, then hurried away.

"Old Sickly looked pleased to see us," I joked, bouncing onto Luke's bed. "Doesn't she ever switch off that ridiculous grin? Maybe her false teeth are too big for her mouth." I roared with laughter, rolling over to clutch Luke's legs, which were thrashing in all directions under the cover.

One glance at Luke's face stopped me, mid-roll.

Jordan looked distressed. Her whisper was fierce. "Oh, shut up, Aaron. Can't you see he's not well?"

Luke spoke, dribbling like mad. "I . . . I'm okay." His head swung from side to side. "You . . . you never made me cry inside before . . . and it . . . hurts."

I felt like he'd hit me right in the stomach. I reached for a tissue and dabbed at his froth. "I'm sorry. I . . . didn't think."

Jordan shook her head, glaring at the ceiling. "Do you ever?"

Luke's limbs slowed. "I'd be dead by now, if Cicely hadn't helped me through all the bad stuff." He gasped, struggling to get the words out. "The only way I know about love is through her . . . and . . ." His voice went quiet. "And you two."

Jordan and I traveled home in silence. I couldn't even eat the brownies. I had this squirming going on inside—like I wanted to start the past hour all over again.

By our next visit, Luke had forgotten my mistake. He was like that—never dwelling on things. But as the winter months dragged on, we watched his health get worse until I could hardly bear to visit. I guessed what was coming.

When he died in December, a week before Christmas, the miserable feeling deep inside me wouldn't let go.

Jordan helped me recover. We talked it through one Sunday after church.

"He found his paradise, Aaron."

"With mountains?"

"Oh yes, I hope so. He was climbing mountains all his life. Tougher ones than we'll ever face."

I sighed. "Yeah. I guess he really lived on a higher level than the rest of us."

Jordan stared at me, eyes dancing. "You mean one without sarcasm? A different planet?"

I swiped at her, and she dodged, laughing.

Perhaps she was right. Maybe wave lengths didn't have to be the same to be comfortable. Jordan's next words brought me up sharp.

"Do you think Luke's watching out for us? You know—keeping an eye on us to see what we make of our lives?"

I didn't answer, but I made up my mind about something as we walked down the road that day. I was going to find a better way to be cool. When I met Luke again, I wanted to be on his level.

Chapter 11

Please, No Zits!

(Sutton Coldfield, England)

"But I never know what to say around boys. No one ever asks me for a date. Anyway . . ." Dawn sniffed. "I'm too busy to bother with parties." She scooped her wavy black hair into a knot behind her head and pinned it in place.

Her friend, Amelia, sighed and shook her head, her blonde curls bobbing. They sat in the changing room after PE. As the only church members in school, they spent plenty of time together.

Amelia's voice rose with each word. "Why can't you see it? You're such a super person—and I love your wacky sense of humor. But if you don't come to church socials, the boys will *never* find out more about you."

"Give me a break. Look at me properly for once. 'Nicely rounded,' my mum calls my figure. 'Fat,' I call it. I barely made it round the running track today. And then there are my eyes. Without glasses I'm lost." Dawn pulled her shoes from the locker. "I can't afford the right clothes, and I get too many zits." She finished putting on her shoes and stood. "Why do you think I can't find a part-time job? I mean—who'd hire *me*?"

Amelia sat, opened-mouthed.

Dawn laughed and quickly added. "It's okay. No worries. I've managed for sixteen years, so you can stop trying to change me."

"I'll stop if you promise something."

"Depends. You have a way of making complicated things sound simple. A promise could mean anything." Dawn braced her shoulders, heading for the door.

Amelia giggled. "This one's easy." She jumped up and rushed after her friend.

They bumped to a halt in front of the main school door. Amelia opened it, letting Dawn go first.

"All you need to do," Amelia said, "is come with me Friday after next to the church Christmas dance in Birmingham. There's a bus going from here."

Dawn marched ahead. "Not me."

Amelia wailed, running after her. "Wait a minute. Listen. I only want to help." She slid to a stop on the icy pavement, and they waited for a gap in the traffic. "Look. If I promise never, ever to pester again, can you at least give it one try? Please?" Amelia placed a hand on her friend's arm.

They crossed the street in silence, then Dawn slowed down. She sighed. "You're not going to believe me, whatever I say, are you?" She lifted her shoulders, then let them drop. "Okay, you win. This once. But you'll wish you hadn't."

Amelia put an arm around her friend and squeezed hard. "It'll be great. And I'll stay with you. If you don't get asked to dance, then I won't dance." She skipped ahead, swinging her backpack from one hand to the other. Then, turning swiftly, she added, "If you like, I can help you decide what to wear. Now, what can we do with your hair? You could wear it down for once—long and—"

"I can sort myself out, thank you," Dawn interrupted, eyes rolling. "Now drop it."

"But—"

"Amelia! I'm warning you . . ."

"I only—"

"There's the bus. Run!"

* * *

That night Dawn did not sleep well. Her prayers took longer than usual. When sleep still wouldn't come at 1:00 a.m., she slipped out of bed and onto her knees for the second time.

"Look," she begged, whispering into the covers. "I'm really not asking for big miracles, like instant weight loss or new eyes or anything like that. But I can't stay a social misfit forever. There's no money for new clothes because of Joe's mission, and no time left for more job hunting. So please, oh please, could there at least be no zits on Friday? And *please* help me have a bit of confidence around boys. Oh, and I did mention, didn't I? Please . . . no zits!"

For the next five days Dawn's stomach heaved every time she heard the word "dance."

Amelia didn't help. She didn't hide her excitement, but rushed onto the bus Wednesday morning and thumped into the empty seat next to Dawn.

Dawn groaned. "Don't say it, Amelia. If you even mention Friday, I'll throw up."

"As if. Anyway, you're silly to get in such a state. It's supposed to be fun. You know—something you do to relax."

"Not for me it isn't. I've been drinking gallons of water all week. Mum says it'll get rid of zits. And I've practiced imaginary conversations with boys when no one's around. Except Monday someone was." She pulled a face. "Our Dave came in the front room as I beamed into the mirror saying, 'And what brings *you* out in zits? Water works wonders for mine.' He thought I'd freaked."

Amelia giggled. "You're not really planning on saying that, are you?"

"As if. But you know me. I'll probably say something equally dreadful."

"Listen. Come to my house after school, and we'll practice social talk. Okay?"

"But what if—?"

"It's okay. No one's home early Wednesdays. Don't worry."

"All right." Dawn breathed deep. "Anything's better than what I've been through these last few days."

Amelia grinned, patting Dawn's arm. "You won't feel half so bad if you have things to say already in your head."

Dawn pushed her glasses firmly on her nose. "I'll try. But if it's a total disaster, I'll know I'm doomed for life."

* * *

Doom came early Thursday evening. Dawn had planned a final visit to Amelia's for a hair makeover. Amelia's family would be out for an hour. But as Dawn was leaving the house, Mum yelled from the kitchen where she was preparing a meal for the missionaries. "Dawn! Wait!"

Mum rushed into the hall, her normal placid features hot and flustered. "I thought I had everything, but there aren't enough eggs for the soufflé." She held out a handful of coins. "Can you go to Walmart on your bike . . . *please?*"

Dawn managed a tight smile. "On my way." She let herself into the garage through the back door, calling over one shoulder. "Don't forget checkouts are slow this time of day. I'll be as quick as I can." She struggled to stay calm. "Can you call Amelia and tell her I can't make it?"

Dawn was far from calm inside. She peddled fast, panting. Was she out of shape or what? She wobbled as a truck overtook too close. Anyway, who cared if she didn't have a classy hairdo? She hunched her shoulders into the blustery wind, glad for once that she wore glasses. At least her eyes stayed open—as long as the lenses didn't steam up.

The busy store was hot and overpowering after the cold ride. Smells of fresh bread followed her as she hurried through the store. At the checkout, everything slowed down. She joined the shuffling queue and took off her coat, slinging it across her shopping cart.

She was standing there, thinking about the dance, when a sudden loud crash made her jump. She felt something touch her, but thought nothing of it because the store was one big noise with people pushing past all the time.

Then an elderly lady pointed at Dawn's jeans. "Will you look at that! Well I never! And the feller ran off! Didn't even stop to apologize, he didn't!" She poked the man next to her. "Don't know what the world's coming to, Albert, really I don't. Imagine leaving all that mess." She edged her own cart farther to the left, shaking her head in disgust.

The woman's attention returned to Dawn. "You all right, deary? I should call the supervisor if I were you." Catching sight of someone in uniform, she raised her arm, wiggling it back and forth, her thin voice rising. "Miss! Miss! Over here. Emergency!"

By now massing customers surrounded Dawn, pushing to get a closer view. The supervisor fought her way through. She looked tired, as if one more problem would be too many.

"What's going on?" She moved closer to Dawn, surveying the scene. "What happened?"

"I think it's paint. It—"

The old lady interrupted. "I saw everything, Miss, I did. See all those tins of paint?" She pointed a shaky finger at nearby shelves. "A man knocked into them, and they toppled all over." Her eyes widened. "One of the lids burst open, and this poor girl got splattered. Then the man took off, he did, quick as you fancy. Never saw anything like—"

"Thank you," the supervisor said, holding up her hand and frowning at the woman. She wore a badge with the name Cheryl in black letters. "You've been a big help." She gave a tense smile. "We'll get this cleaned up at once."

She turned to Dawn, who by this time was pink with embarrassment. "Sorry about the mess," Cheryl said. "Not something we could help, mind you. Nevertheless, we must accept liability. Let's see. Besides the cart and floor, how much of your clothing's affected?"

Dawn glanced down at the only pair of jeans she possessed, and the tee shirt she planned to wear to the dance—both ruined.

"Uh . . . these are pretty bad, aren't they?" Her lips quivered. She clamped them tight.

"Hmm! Definitely a claims case. Might take a week or two, but we can lend you a staff uniform to get you home. I think the young lady who left today was about your size." She reached behind a counter and pulled out a navy blue dress, eyeing Dawn's shape. "There. Looks perfect. Now come with me, and you can try it on." She picked the pack of eggs from the cart, handing them to Dawn. "No need to pay for these."

Dawn followed Cheryl in a daze—until something the woman said sunk in. *Someone left today.* She wanted to ask if the position had been filled, but Cheryl didn't slow until they reached the office at the back of the store.

Cheryl opened a door, saying, "See if the uniform fits, then come to my office and we can fill in the claim forms."

Dawn opened her mouth to speak, but Cheryl had already moved on. Dawn shut the door and removed her paint-stained clothing.

The uniform fit better than anything she owned. The dark navy even made her look slimmer. She drew in a breath and gazed in the mirror, imagining herself standing behind a checkout, punching in numbers. Could she do it? She'd have to get used to talking to people. But hey, why not? Amelia would help her practice.

Dawn was so caught up in her newfound resolve that it came as a shock to hear Cheryl's voice right outside the door.

"Is that dress the right size?"

Dawn wanted to say something about the job right then, before she lost her nerve, but her mouth went dry. She opened the door. "Thanks, yes, it fits perfect. I . . . I . . ."

Cheryl looked her over and nodded. "Good. Now let's see about these forms."

Dawn followed her to a desk in a nearby room, and they both sat. She held her breath, waiting for Cheryl to stop writing, praying the right words would come out.

Cheryl looked up. "Your full name?"

"Dawn Dixon. I'd like to—"

"Address?"

"I live at . . ." Dawn took a breath, then the words tumbled out. "Look, I'd really like to work here part-time. I've tried before, but someone always beat me to it. You have a vacancy, and I fit the dress. Please, will you give me a chance, seeing as I'm here? And you most likely need help, and I promise to work hard, and—"

"Just a minute," Cheryl said, waving her hand. "One thing at a time." Then she raised her head and peered at Dawn, tapping her pen against her teeth. "You know, it might work. The Christmas rush starts soon, and we do need extra staff."

She pulled another form from a drawer and pushed it toward Dawn. "Here, fill this in while we answer these other questions. We'll give you a trial run starting Saturday morning."

Dawn stared at Cheryl. "Really? Hey, thanks . . . thanks very much."

"One more thing," Cheryl said. "What about the ruined clothes? I can throw them away, if you like."

An idea entered Dawn's head—one that made her smile. "I'll take them with me."

Her phone call to Amelia twenty minutes later came out in such a rush that her friend was confused.

"An old lady in a paint shop did *what*?"

"No, no. It was Walmart, and it was a man . . ." Dawn took a shaky breath. "Listen. Basically, I'm up in the air because I have a job starting Saturday. One problem—my clothes for tomorrow are covered in paint."

"Oh! But Dawn—"

"Hold on! You haven't heard the best bit. I can put all those things you told me to the test. You know—sense of humor, whatever."

"You mean you're still coming? Paint and all?"

"Exactly. If you're right, then what's on the outside won't stop me having a good time—okay?"

Amelia was silent. Then excitement broke through. "Know what? I'll wear mine, too. The ones I lent my brother when he decorated his bedroom." She laughed. "Everyone will ask questions."

"Yeah. And—get this—I only have one zit left."

"If it's still there tomorrow, you could always splat paint over it."

"Naaah. It might grow bigger."

As they walked in the dance hall next evening, their laughter attracted stares. A group soon gathered, and introductions began.

During a quiet moment later in the evening, Dawn whispered to Amelia, "You were right. It's not so hard to relax. They love the paint story. And guess what?"

Amelia's eyes shimmered. "Don't tell me. Someone gave you the magic cure for zits?"

"Nope."

"What then?"

"I have a date!"

Chapter 12

Okay to Cheat?

(Provo, Utah, USA)

Cody slammed his bedroom door, looked at the stack of books on his bed, and let out his breath through clenched teeth. Then he leaned across the navy-blue comforter and shut the blind against a dark winter sky. Next he flipped on the desk light and dropped onto the swivel chair, letting his head sink between his hands.

It took a moment for the music coming from his brother's room to penetrate his brain, but when it did, he jumped up, crossed the floor in three steps, and yanked the door open again.

"Cut the volume, Brendan!" he yelled down the hall. "I've got a big test tomorrow."

The brass and drums didn't change.

Cody marched his tall, lean frame down the hallway and banged on Brendan's door. "Cut it. I can't study."

The door cracked open, and Brendan's grinning, chubby face appeared at floor level. He was eleven years old, the youngest of five Rendyke boys, and often up to mischief. Nothing rattled his life—bossy seventeen-year-old brother included.

Cody edged his foot against Brendan's chin. "Get up, you nerd, and fix the noise."

"You missed something."

"You'll be missing something in a minute—like a nose and some teeth."

"What about please? Mom says—"

"I'm counting to three—"

"Okay, okay!" Brendan shuffled backward along the floor, and his door drifted open. Cody watched papers scrunching as his brother wriggled on his stomach over the drawings, making his way to a CD player perched on top of his bookcase.

Cody felt a twinge of conscience. "So what's with all the paper anyway? And why are you down there? You decorating the floor or something?"

Brendan scrambled to his feet and hit the off switch with his right hand. "Nope." He swung around. "Got this art homework. Mr. Trendler wants something big to cover the music-room walls for a concert. Our art group got the job. Have to do the groundwork. Get it? On the ground?"

Cody ignored the wisecrack. "But you just ruined it."

Brendan shrugged. "That's okay. It's only practice. Getting ideas." He leapt onto his bed and bounced. "Tomorrow we splash paint on massive sheets of paper. And guess what?"

Cody folded his arms and leaned against the door. "They paint you and hang you on the wall?"

"That girl you like in your class—Madeline? She and some other art seniors get to help us."

"I don't like her." Cody ran his fingers across his forehead. "Besides, she wouldn't look twice at me—not with this week's breakout."

"I'll tell her my zit-face brother wants a date."

Cody's arms unfolded fast. "Get lost, Brendan! One word about me, and you're—"

Brendan butted in, pulling a face. "Hey Madeline," he said in a gruff voice. "My brother and I have the same knock-out looks. If you like me, you'll love—"

He got no further. Cody was across the room before Brendan opened his eyes. The boys' laughter and shouts echoed through the house as blankets, pillows, and paper flew in all directions.

Mom's voice floated up from the kitchen. "Thought you two had homework. If you have time to mess around, you can come and do dishes."

Brendan gave Cody one last push in the arm. "Yeah. Go do dishes, big brother."

Cody sighed and straightened his khaki colored sweatshirt. "I'd rather do anything than study for that math test tomorrow."

"You'll be fine, Cody. You always are." Brendan sniffed, wriggling his feet free from his bed sheet. "Wish I was like you. Math creeps me out."

Cody grinned and cuffed his small brother on the shoulder. "Problem is I put this off too long. Should have studied instead of going to the Cougar game last night. Now I don't know where to begin."

Brendan's head tipped to one side, and his eyebrows rose. "What about prayer? That's what they always say."

"Hmmm. Not sure it works like that. I'm supposed to *do* something before I pray."

"Yep. Like me doing all this for art." Brendan's arm swept wide. "Want me to test you?"

Cody got to his feet and headed for the door. He spoke over his shoulder. "Thanks, kid, but this math is way over your head." He closed Brendan's door, muttering, "Way over mine, too."

* * *

Mr. Franklin, the math teacher, surveyed the classroom. His head ached, and his mouth was dry, and the math test was only half way through. He'd sat at his desk, checking on the class and trying to concentrate on tomorrow's lesson preparation, for what felt like hours.

The room was warm and stuffy—the only sound a constant shuffling of papers, a few coughs, and an occasional buzz from a semi-dormant fly as it batted against the long wall of windows.

Mr. Franklin felt his eyelids closing, his head nodding. He pulled up straight, rubbing his eyes and then stared around the room. All heads were down. His own head dipped again.

Mr. Franklin had no idea how long he dozed, but an escaping snore jolted him upright once more.

It was then he saw something disturbing. Cody Rendyke

appeared to be looking over the shoulder of Jim Taite, who was writing left-handed, leaning on his right elbow, with his head resting on his hand.

Mr. Franklin took a deep breath, wide-awake now. *Not Cody. Surely not Cody Rendyke.*

Five minutes later, the bell rang. Mr. Franklin collected the papers, dismissing the class. One hour of school remained to check this out and deal with the problem—if there was one. He sifted through the pile and found both Cody and Jim's tests. It didn't take long to discover they matched perfectly. His chest tightened as he sixed up what must be done. How he loathed dealing with cheats. He walked into the corridor and signaled a passing student.

"Find Cody Rendyke. Tell him Mr. Franklin wants to see him in Room H as soon as school ends."

* * *

Forty minutes later, Cody stood in the corridor rubbing his palms, now sticky with sweat. He heard his heartbeat thudding in his ears, and his stomach felt like it was shooting knives at his throat. He dragged his feet toward Mr. Franklin's table.

"Ah, Cody. I have a question for you."

Cody remained silent, his breathing shaky.

"Your test answers—both right and wrong—are the same as the boy who sat in front of you. Jim Taite."

Cody took a sharp breath.

The teacher continued. "Were you cheating, Cody?"

The answer shot out. "No!"

Mr. Franklin frowned, the wrinkles under his brown eyes folding in deep lines. "I see." He coughed. "Then how do you account for—?"

"Must be because . . . Jim and I, we study together. We work the same way."

"Uh-huh." The teacher didn't sound convinced. "I thought I saw you looking over Jim's shoulder this afternoon. You sure you weren't copying his work?"

"I wouldn't do that. No, I was checking to see if he was okay. He looked kind of sleepy."

"Yes. It was warm in here. I felt myself nodding a few times."

"I saw you. I mean, you looked like . . . um . . . what I'm saying is that you weren't out for long . . ."

"I want to trust you, Cody. I really do. But I don't feel good about this. All evidence points toward cheating."

Cody felt pressure building in his temples. "Please believe me. I'm a top seminary student. I never miss a church meeting. I'm not the kind of person to . . . to cheat."

By now, Cody's cheeks were flushed. He spoke fast. "One of the teachers, Mrs. Snow, she's in my ward. The Young Women's president. She'll tell you."

Mr. Franklin rose to his feet. "This is most difficult. But I don't want to make a mistake. It's far too serious, and so are the consequences. I want you to stay here while I see if Mrs. Snow's still in the staff room."

* * *

The door swung on its hinges. Cody, legs trembling, moved to a nearby desk and sat down. *This can't be happening. What will Mom say? She'll never believe it. And the rest of the family—especially Brendan—he won't understand. What was it he said?* He pictured the boy's cheeky grin for a moment. *What about prayer—that's what he said.*

But prayer wouldn't come. He couldn't get the words to form in his mind. Cody felt tears coming and closed his eyes again, letting his head drop onto his hands—clenched tight on the desktop. This time, desperation drove him to speak out loud.

"Please, Heavenly Father. I'm so sorry I cheated. Please, I promise, I'll never do it again, if you'll only help me . . . *please.*"

He raised his eyes and stared in front, seeing nothing, hearing nothing, totally absorbed in the pain of his confused mind.

Mr. Franklin's shoes striking the wooden classroom floor brought Cody to attention. He held his breath, not looking at the teacher.

Mr. Franklin's voice was dull. "Well, young man. I've talked to Mrs. Snow, and you're very fortunate. She says she knows and respects you and your family, and is certain you'd never cheat." He stared at Cody for a few moments, and then slapped the test papers onto the desktop, making Cody jump. Mr. Franklin spoke quietly. "You're free to go home."

Cody blinked and his voice came out thick. "Thank you, Mr. Franklin. Thank you."

He left the classroom, trying not to run down the long, empty, echoing corridor.

* * *

The following day, Mr. Franklin arrived at school early. His headache the night before had developed into a migraine, and he couldn't finish marking the mound of test papers at home.

He dropped the papers on his desk and walked to the window overlooking the playground. A few students crossed the square, congregating in small groups, despite the cold. The sun already shone, but today it didn't help him feel good the way it normally did. Returning to his desk, he slumped into his chair, running his hand through his hair.

He'd marked a few papers when a hesitant knock sounded on his classroom door. He looked up in surprise.

"Come in, Madeline. What are you doing here this early?"

Madeline Summers hesitated. Then she edged into the room. "Mr. Franklin . . ."

"Come and sit down," he said. "What's on your mind?"

"This is really hard for me but, I had to come. I wouldn't normally do such a thing, but . . ."

Mr. Franklin leaned forward, resting his elbows on the test papers, taking in the girl's appearance. Her short, black curls were tangled, and her grey eyes bloodshot. "Go on, Madeline. How can I help you?"

The girl looked down at her twisting hands. It was obvious tears weren't far away. "I need to tell you something. I've worried about it all night. Even prayed about it over and over, and in the end decided there's no other way. I have to tell you."

"And?"

Madeline squirmed in her chair. Then she raised her chin, looking Mr. Franklin in the eye. "I was late leaving my art class last night. We had extra stuff to prepare for a group of younger kids we helped yesterday. I walked past your room on my way out, and I had a really strong feeling I should look in. But . . . but I couldn't go through the door."

She hesitated, biting her full lower lip. "It was open, but there was this boy sitting alone at a desk, and he was talking—praying out loud." Her face crumpled as she forced out the next words in a high whisper. "It was Cody Rendyke."

Mr. Franklin sucked in air. He handed the girl a tissue from a box on his desk. "What was he praying about?"

She blew her nose and then wiped her eyes with her fingers. "He . . . he confessed he'd cheated, and asked the Lord for help." Her voice rose, and she spoke faster. "I was upset and crept away so he wouldn't see me, and worried about it all the way home. I didn't know what to do. I kept thinking, Cody wouldn't cheat—but what if he really did, and what if he's never found out, and he thinks cheating's okay. It could mess up his life."

Mr. Franklin rose and moved toward Madeline, patting her shoulder. "You did the right thing. Thank you. You've solved a problem that's worried me since yesterday." He indicated the door with his hand. "I'll take it from here. Don't you worry any more."

The tearful girl walked away, and Mr. Franklin shook his head, returning to his desk. He glanced at the clock on the far wall, working out the best time to deal with Cody.

* * *

It was noon break before Mr. Franklin called Cody to the front of class as the other students left. "I'd like you to stay a moment, Cody. We need to talk."

Cody's face went red. He stuffed his hands deep in his jeans' pockets.

He'd not slept the night before, but spent hours going over everything that happened. He couldn't believe how easy it was adding lies to his mistake—or how bad guilt felt—even though he'd got away with it.

Or had he? What if he was found out? What if he wasn't, and it tortured him like this for the rest of his life? But other people got away with far worse things, and nothing happened to them. Or did it? What if they still went through midnight torture and never told anyone?

On the other hand, the thought of telling the truth now made him want to throw up.

Why, oh why did I do it? It's not worth all this. He wanted to pray away the darkness and confusion, but how could he? He'd already messed up big time by asking for something he shouldn't have. By three o'clock in the morning he'd tossed around so much he ached all over. He'd jumped out of bed and knelt against the soft covers, pouring out his sorrow to his Father, pleading forgiveness.

"It's bad news, Cody," Mr. Franklin began. "Bad news for both of us. I can't stand cheating, but dishonesty is even worse."

Cody raised his head, stunned at the twisted sense of relief flooding his body. So he wasn't getting away with it after all. "How did you—?"

"Never mind how. The point is you cheated not only me and Mrs. Snow, but also yourself and your family. You let everyone down. How can I ever trust you again?"

Cody stared at the floor, unable to think of anything to say that wouldn't sound lame.

Mr. Franklin slapped the desktop, his voice rising. "I'm giving you a zero on this test. It's up to you how you explain it to your parents. But I hope you've learned something from all this, and that you have the courage to tell them the truth. Better they face disappointment now and work with you, than wonder where things went wrong later."

The teacher stood and paced the floor, his long face stern, bushy eyebrows meeting in the middle. He glanced at Cody, who was fighting back tears.

Mr. Franklin lowered his voice. "I really don't think you're a bad person. But if you get away with this, you'll always wonder if it's okay to cheat. I promise you that it is *not*. It's the beginning of a dishonest life that could lead to problems you can't even imagine—problems that can destroy a marriage, a career, and eventually you. For everyone's sake, let it end right here."

He stopped pacing and gave Cody's shoulder a squeeze, followed by a gentle push toward the door. "Now go get some lunch. And don't make me do this again. Not ever."

Cody slouched toward the door, then turned to face Mr. Franklin, speaking in a low voice. "I'm so sorry."

He left the room and headed down the hallway and out through a side door. He crossed the parking area and turned into the street, quickening his pace, wishing he could catch a bus to another city far away. His stomach was too knotted for food, and he didn't want to speak to another person for a long, long time.

He'd turned off University Avenue and was wandering down Center Street, when he got the feeling he was being followed. It didn't make sense, because each time he looked around, the few people walking were unfamiliar and about their business. He shrugged it off and went on, wishing he'd grabbed his coat before leaving the building. Weak sunshine between clouds did nothing to keep out the bitter cold.

He prayed again as he walked, and then his thoughts turned to his family. There was no running away from them—they had to know sooner or later because he couldn't deal with this burning up inside much longer. He took a deep breath. That was it. He'd go tell them how sorry he was, and do it right now.

He made an about-turn and bumped into someone coming up behind.

She squealed. It was Madeline Summers.

Cody's yelp was one of horror more than fright. *What is she doing here?*

She looked almost as pitiful as he felt. Her face was all tear-stained, and those big eyes full of shame. "I'm sorry, Cody, really sorry. I saw you leave, and I guessed what happened . . . and . . . and followed you, in case—"

"What are you talking about? How could you possibly guess anything?"

She bit her lip. "Can we get out of the cold? There's something I . . . have to tell you."

This was unbelievable. The terrible sorrow he'd felt turned into full-blown alarm.

They walked into a coffee shop, and Cody dug in his pocket for change. There was enough for one hot chocolate. They sat at a table, and Cody waited while Madeline grabbed a napkin from a box on the table and dabbed her eyes.

"You're going to hate me," she began, dropping her gaze to the green-tiled table top. The drink arrived, and Cody pushed it toward Madeline. But she ignored the steaming mug and went on talking in a low voice. "I was there when you prayed yesterday . . . in Mr. Franklin's room."

His mind flipped, and a chill passed through him that even hot chocolate couldn't reach. He tried to speak, but words wouldn't come. He dipped his chin, unable to look anywhere but down.

Then she did something that froze him to the seat. She reached out and touched his hands that lay clasped on the table. "You feel awful, Cody. I'm so sorry." Then she explained the whole story, right up to her meeting with Mr. Franklin.

Cody sat there, unable to do anything except blink. A moment later, he shook his head and looked her in the eye, hunching his shoulders against the misery. "All I can say is that I've never cheated before, and I never will again—not ever."

She gave him a watery smile, and Cody saw himself reflected in her eyes.

"I guessed that about you," she said. "That's why I had to tell Mr. Franklin—even though I didn't want to. It was the hardest thing I've ever done. Can you forgive me?"

His stomach unknotted. He even managed a short laugh, the relief was so intense. "I seriously think that's the wrong way around. What if you forgive me . . . and I thank you?"

She smiled again.

Then Cody remembered something, and the good feelings vanished. "Uh-oh! My parents. I still have to tell them."

Melilnda reached for the mug that no longer steamed. "I'll come with you, if you want me to. We can explain together." She sipped the drink and then offered the mug to Cody. "Want to share?"

He took a mouthful, savoring the warm sweetness.

The moment of truth never tasted so good.

Chapter 13

Beyond the Thorns

(London, England)

Justin hunted through the canes for a decent raspberry, passing over spoiled berries with perfect fronts and bird-pecked backs until he found a beauty. He picked it from the bush, his mouth watering—until he saw the bug scrambling out from its hiding place deep inside the fruit.

Flinging the raspberry to the ground in disgust, he squashed it underfoot with sharp jabs, feeling rebellion rising in his chest. Why was everything so flaky? Family, friends, life . . . and a mission. The last word twisted in his mind, bleeding in and out like the red raspberry stain spreading between the cracks on the old paving slab at his feet.

Justin frowned. Didn't he always know a mission would get here some day? He punched the nearest leaves. How could so many years of preparation leave him feeling like this—cheated and scared? Two years of life thrown away. Right here in England! He wasn't even going overseas, for crying out loud.

He stuffed his fists into his jeans pockets, scuffing the dead berry with the toe of his shoe. Non-member friends got jobs, cars, and girls. Nothing like serving and sticking to rules. He *was* worthy to go, but what fun would it be walking around in a black suit for two years?

Then panic replaced anger. Was the Church worth all this sacrifice? He felt like he was on a motorway at night with lights snaking off into the distance. He couldn't see where they headed—or if he was even on the right road.

He looked up and saw his mum heading for the fruit garden. *Oh no, not again. Not another motherly chat.* But there was no escape.

Mum's cheerful smile did nothing for his bad mood. "I'm glad you're here, Justin. I'm in a hurry and need your help picking gooseberries."

"Okay, okay." Justin sighed, steeling himself for the advice he was sure would come.

Mum handed him a plastic bowl and began filling her own, fingers moving with care between the greenery, uncovering fat and hairy fruit.

Justin scowled at the bushes. He flicked the leaves with his fingers. "What's the point," he muttered. "There's nothing here."

"It takes a bit of searching, dear. They're camouflaged. You have to look deeper."

Justin gritted his teeth, waiting for the next words. He wasn't disappointed.

"Like missionaries," she said. "You know, never giving up."

Justin rolled his eyes. How did Mum find missionary work in everything they did? He thrust his fingers further into the bush, then yelled and jumped away nursing a bleeding thumb.

"That bush has thorns," he yelled. "That's it. I'm out of here."

His mother spoke calmly. "I'll only be a minute, if you hold this for me." She handed him her bowl and dropped in a big green berry. "It's surprising how much people can be like prize gooseberries. They hide behind a prickly skin, but with enough love they change. You'll find some like that on your mission."

Justin muttered between clenched teeth, "I don't want to talk about this."

Mum was already weaving her way between bushes. She glanced over her shoulder. "What was that, dear?"

"Nothing."

* * *

When the day for Justin's last sacrament meeting finally arrived, he still wasn't happy. Sacrifice was not his favorite word.

"This fine, upstanding young man, Elder Justin Tomlinson," the bishop was saying, "is about to exchange two years of his life for something out of this world."

Justin's thoughts spun as he sat on the stand, dreading his turn to speak. He didn't want to be out of this world. And what about Andy and Phil down there? They were nineteen and refused to go. Why didn't he stop all this and say no? He looked at his family sitting on the front row smiling at him. Mum and Dad looked proud. Jeff, Brittany, and Pete—their eyes were big with hero worship. And little David and Meg, the twins, sat open-mouthed—quiet for a change.

Justin moved to the rostrum, amazed his legs worked. With dry mouth and perspiring hands, he stumbled through his talk. "And although I'm not sure why I'm going," he concluded, "I suppose . . . I mean . . . no, I *am* going because the prophet said all young men should serve, and because my family and I follow the prophet."

Justin returned to his seat, dazed, wondering where those words came from and if he really said them.

* * *

The following week, outside the Missionary Training Center, Dad hugged Justin. "First time I've felt like crying in years, son," he said.

With Dad's arm around his shoulder, Justin gazed up at the temple. His vision blurred.

Two hours later he wanted those minutes with Dad back. There were things he wanted to say—like, "I love you, Dad. You're the greatest. Thanks for everything, Dad. I'll get through this." But it was too late to do anything other than get on with MTC life.

In the whirl of learning that followed, Justin's testimony grew powerful, and the road ahead became clear. Until it was time to leave. Then doubts began all over again.

It was his first assignment in the London mission field that caused a major problem. He stared at his new companion. Was this some kind of sick joke? The man looked like a boxer, a heavyweight. Talk about muscles. And that huge, flattened nose. Who in their right senses would open the door if they saw *him* standing there?

"Hey, Elder Tomlinson. I'm Elder Warriner from Texas." The man's smile warmed his square face with its out-jutting jaw. But that handshake—Justin thought his fingers would never be normal again. He responded with a grunt. How could he ever get along with Elder Warriner?

Justin soon found out. Elder Warriner never stopped working. The man's energy and excitement were exhausting. There was no time to feel sorry for himself, or wish he was anywhere else. Even family and friends began to fade as new people became part of Jason's life.

Several weeks later, they were in a run-down London back street where the houses stood in a row, no gaps between, and no yard in front. The tall window frames next to a solid front door showed flaking brown paint that looked like it left the paint can a hundred years ago.

Several moments passed after Justin's knock before heavy footsteps sounded inside the house.

"Yeah?" The snarling man hitched up sloppy, grey trousers, and thrust the door wide with his elbow. He was massive. A soggy cigarette dangled from half-closed lips, and a beer can looked ready to make a fast exit from his fist in the direction of the Elders.

"Good morning." Elder Warriner's smile clipped corners off the man's invisible barrier. At least that's what Justin told himself, watching the beer can lower and the man's eyes narrow.

"We're from The Church of Jesus Christ of Latter-day Saints, and we'd like to share a message with you."

The man's eyes widened. He sniffed hard, wiping ash off his unshaven chin with his knuckles.

"Uh . . . huh. Thought you were the TV license spies. What you want then?" He stared at Elder Warriner's craggy features.

"You a boxer or something? Used to do a bit of boxing meself. Well, come in then. Could do with a change from the telly."

They followed the man down a dark hallway. Justin noticed peeling wallpaper, frayed carpet, and the smell of damp chips and vinegar. What was the point of even talking to this man? He poked Elder Warriner and mouthed "No way." A Texan eye winked back.

"Me name's Floyd," their host announced. Then, pointing to a frail woman hunched by the gas fire, he said. "This is me missus, Elspeth, and them's me kids—Jimmy, Jane, Sally, and Thelma." Four pairs of eyes flicked from TV, to Elders, to TV.

Justin gazed at the thin foursome. The man actually sounded proud of them. Into Justin's mind flashed a picture of his mum. How she'd love to take them home and fatten them up.

Floyd looked at the children and pointed to Elder Warriner. "This 'ere man's a boxer. Take a look at his face now. Your Uncle Bert looked like that when he left for Canada." Floyd took on a sparring position, his big frame blocking the light and his weight shifting to his toes, hands held in loose fists. He flung a question at Elder Warriner. "Where you been boxing then, lad?"

"Um . . . Floyd." Elder Warriner was solemn. "We have something more important to talk about than boxing. I used to box every day in boys' clubs back home, and I was pretty good. But I gave that up to come here and share a message with you."

Floyd looked puzzled, then suspicious. "Are you chicken, or something?" He began moving toward the door, his face surly again. "No time for sissies."

Justin scrambled to his feet, giving a let's-move-it eyebrow signal to his companion. But before Justin could step forward, he heard his own voice speaking, though he'd no idea why. "By the way, Floyd, is your mother important to you?"

The words quivered in the silence. Justin's mind did a swift-action replay. For a brief second he was in his own garden picking gooseberries, hearing mum talk all over again.

Justin jumped as Floyd took a step in his direction.

"What do you know about me ma?" the big man asked. With neck pushed forward, his head looked even more unfriendly. But his tone softened as he paced the floor. "Me little ma, oh, she was right lovely, was me little ma." His face took on a tender sadness.

Justin glanced at the children, whose gaze at last had left the flickering screen.

Tears dribbled down Floyd's cheeks. "I was a lad of fifteen when she died."

Little Thelma jumped up and ran to her dad. She hugged him as far around his belly as her thin arms could reach.

The effect was startling. Scooping her into his arms, Floyd held her close, patting her back. "I still think of me ma every night before going to sleep. Her life was tough, but I always knew she loved every hair on me 'ead."

Floyd focused on the Elders. He squinted at Justin's face. "Lad, if you can tell me where me ma is now, then that's something I want to know." He motioned to his wife. "Let's see a bit of that fire, Elspeth. How about a cup of tea for these boys? And you kids hitch up on that sofa. Give the lads a seat."

While Elder Warriner explained why tea wasn't an option, a thought dropped into Justin's mind—it was the motorway thing again, only this time it was different. This time, he saw where it was heading. He joined in the discussion, backing up his companion's words with his own testimony that bubbled out, getting stronger and stronger.

* * *

Floyd and his family were baptized six weeks later. Baptism day brought a radiant family—washed, mended, and smiling.

Floyd's big hand squeezed Justin's shoulder when the service ended. "Lad, I can't find words to thank you and your mate for all you taught us. You've given us something to live for." He sniffed and tilted his head upward. "You're a cracking bit of inspiration from up there, you missionaries. Thanks, lads, thanks a million."

Justin shook Floyd's hand and was turning away, overcome by sudden emotion, when Floyd pulled Justin close, enveloping him in the tightest squeeze he'd ever received. That did it. Justin let out a sob, and within seconds they were all crying—including Elder Warriner.

Tears soon turned to laughter. As they all hugged, into Justin's mind flashed another motorway image, only this time the traffic was spinning toward something bright and shiny. Catching another Texan wink from his missionary companion, he had the warm knowledge they were on the right road.

Chapter 14

On Bike-Back

(Finglas, Dublin, Ireland)

I always liked the idea of digging up the family tree and finding some cool ancestor with a romantic story. Not that I didn't appreciate modern romance. I did—until Mark came on the scene.

Mark. Six-foot tall, smooth blond hair, and eyes the colour of Irish grass. He was my idea of male hunk—past, present and future.

One problem. He was my sister's boyfriend.

My sister, Lisa, was also my best friend. At seventeen—a year younger than me—she attracted men like clouds attract moisture. *And* she was soft, blonde, and fluffy with it. I'm the opposite. Skinny, with mousey brown hair, freckles, and an over-generous mouth. Her boyfriends treated me like a sister.

That was fine. I was too young to settle down. But I wouldn't say no to someone like Mark. Anyway, he was the reason I decided to get buried in my roots sooner rather than later. I couldn't hurt Lisa. I'd never seen her so happy. At least all the excitement meant she never noticed me disappear each time they were together. But getting Mark out of my thoughts wasn't easy.

I scrambled for the back door when I heard Mark come in through the front this evening. Mother questioned me from the sink where she stood peeling apples. "So who's the lucky man, Keziah?"

I gasped, thinking she'd guessed something about Mark. "M . . . man?"

She looked at me. "I thought perhaps you were seeing that new convert from the bank in Dublin. What's his name, now . . . ah, yes . . . Giles." She gave a wistful smile. "Perfect for you my dear. And so polite. A charming young man."

I shuddered. All Giles talked about was his new hybrid car and the weather. He never looked me in the eye when we spoke, and he picked his ears with his car key. Not my type at all. Oh for a knight on gleaming horse-back waiting to carry me away. Now that would bring a sparkle to Mum's eyes . . . and mine.

"Sorry." I laughed. "I'm going to the Family History Centre."

"Really, my dear?" She swished water around the stainless steel sink. "That's good because I don't have many names on my mother's side yet. Hope you find someone."

"One of the young men down there is back to the sixteen hundreds in Cork on his father's line."

"I'm so glad there's a young man, my dear." She brushed a length of brown hair behind her ear with wet fingers. "I don't like you going out on your own all the time."

"Adam's not my young man. He's a convert who just moved from Killarney—a history addict. When the Elders told him about genealogy, he couldn't believe his luck." I brushed long bits of fringe out of my eyes. "Nice lad, but not my type."

I kissed her cheek, and from the corner of my eye noticed Mark walk into the kitchen.

I opened the back door. "Have to run, Mum. I'm late."

Mark waved me to stop, grinning. "Want a lift, Keziah? Lisa and I are going to the cinema. There's a crowd of us meeting there."

My heartbeat sounded too loud, and I wished there was a quick cure for hot cheeks.

"No . . . no thank you." I slid round our white wooden door. "It's not cold. I'll be at the chapel in ten minutes. Besides, I need the exercise. Enjoy the film."

I ran. It wasn't far from our semi-detached in the estate off Finglas Road to the chapel. The spring air smelt fresh and scrubbed after a stormy day. I loved how weather did that, like putting a twist in the atmosphere, spinning us in new directions. I breathed deep. I needed some new direction. I had to get Mark out of my head.

The Family History Centre inside Finglas chapel was used for Primary on Sundays, but tonight, equipment was pulled from cupboards. The clicking of film readers and faces reflecting computer screen light gave the place an other-world feeling.

"'Evening, Keziah." Adam's rich voice from across the floor had a soothing effect on my nerves. He couldn't be more than twenty, but was balding already.

I wasn't soothed for long.

Winding film onto the reader was difficult. It was a different machine from last time, and the take-up spool for the other end of the film kept slipping. I wished I'd arrived earlier and grabbed a computer instead.

"Here, let me." Adam appeared, at my elbow. "This one's tricky. You have to make it click into place to stop it sliding around."

I thanked him. If only I could click myself into place like that. Since meeting Mark, my feelings never went in the right direction. Why wasn't I born in a different age when life was simple? I concentrated on the names rolling before me on the screen. Such old, spidery letters. Did the writers have any idea that someone over a hundred years later would try to read their words?

My two hours were nearly up when I found my great-great-grandmother on Mum's side. There she was—Keziah Grover, born in Clonfert, County Galway. *Whoa! I'm named after this one.* She showed as an eighteen-year-old daughter of William and Alice Grover, but there was something odd about the entry.

On looking closer, I realized she was married, but living with her parents. Her husband's name appeared beneath hers. His name was . . . Mark!

I groaned. This was totally unfair. Mark. Again. And married to my great-great-grandmother. All these Marks, and not one of them mine.

Adam's worried voice came over my shoulder. "Are you okay?"

"I'm fine . . . really." My fingers shook. "No, actually, I'm not fine at all." I sighed. "It's a long story." I began rewinding the film, half wishing I hadn't found Keziah.

"Turning that thing makes your arm ache," Adam said. "Let me help."

"Thank you, but no. I need some action after sitting here all evening." Gripping the handle and giving it one last furious twirl, I whisked all those people's names and lives right out of sight.

"Hey, Keziah?" Adam said. "May I walk you home? I don't have a car—only a bike as yet. But that would give us time for your long story." He shot me a questioning grin, head on one side. I noticed for the first time how deep blue his eyes were.

So we walked slowly out of the building, through the car park, and on past the cemetery over the road, talking and talking. It felt odd. It was usually me doing all the listening and giving advice. I liked having it the other way round for a change.

"So you see," I finished, as we reached my house, "I have two choices. I can either leave home and start again somewhere far away, or I can stay and suffer, and maybe make Lisa suffer, too."

We stood. He looked at me for a moment before speaking. "You don't have to, you know."

"Don't have to what?"

"Choose between the two."

I blinked. "I don't?"

"What about a third choice?" He was looking down at his feet now, scuffing the dust round the edge of his bike wheel.

"Huh? I don't have a third."

He straightened, sucking in his breath. "Yes you do. You could be my girlfriend for a while, and . . . and maybe we'd have such a good time that Mark wouldn't seem quite so . . ."

He bit his lip—I guess because I was looking pretty amazed.

Then he plunged on. "I enjoy being with you. Nothing serious, right?"

"Right." I was silent a moment. I guess Adam could never be Mark, but what Adam said made sense. Any distraction helped.

So I nodded, smiling into his eyes. "Thanks. You're a good friend. I like that." I touched his sleeve. "By the way, there I was, looking at all those names at church, and I don't know *your* last name."

"It's Knight," he said. "Adam Knight."

It took a minute to sink in. Then I was helpless with laughter. "I'm sorry. I'm not laughing at you," I said. "I'll have to explain another time. But I think a wish I made earlier just came true—in the craziest way."

He lifted one shoulder, chuckling. "At least you're not sad anymore." He swung one leg over the saddle then peddled away, waving and calling out, "I'll ring you tomorrow."

I pushed open the front door, smiling and humming a tune—wondering if great-great-grandma Keziah saw what had happened and was grinning too. It's good to know that today there are still a few shining Knights around—even if this one did come on bike-back.

Chapter 15

Slicing Rainbows

(Anglesey, North Wales)

"If I could only get from here to there without the bit in the middle, I'd be okay," Kimberly whispered, kneeling on her bed and gazing out the window over the rooftops. "But there are too many miles and too many days." She sighed, sinking onto her heels on the blue and white striped quilt.

A September storm was on the way. A snappy stillness surrounded the houses, outlining them against the fields beyond. Mounds of thick cloud squashed light to the ground, reflecting florescent green.

Strange how a scene could look so different so fast. A bit like Ethan.

Kimberly rested her chin against her hands on the window ledge. Ethan looked very different in his jeans on their farewell date last week, compared to Elder Ethan Williams in his suit, boarding a train for the England London Mission this morning.

"Two years!" she murmured. "How can I possibly get through two endless years?" She blinked twice, determined to stop the tears. She'd managed to keep them away until after the train had gone and Ethan's family left, but walking home through the leafy Welsh lanes brought a flood of memories. She squeezed her eyes shut now, trying not to see the rainbow outside, joining light and dark beyond the fields.

What was it Ethan said about rainbows? "They bring things

together, Kim, if you let them." She heard his voice in her mind—slow, deep, a reliable sound. "Think of them beginning in the eternities and reaching out to us here. If we could catch a slice, it would remind us of heaven."

"To me, it's you at one end, far away, and me at the other end—lonely."

He smiled and reached out, stroking her hair. "We could look for treasure in between, instead of at the end of the rainbow."

She bit her lip, glancing away.

"Hey," he said, turning her face toward him, his touch gentle. "I don't want to think of you sitting around moping. I want you to have a good time. And that means meeting people, dating, having fun."

Kim leaned against him and sighed. "Okay, Ethan. If you say so." But she didn't mean it.

And now he was gone, and life was empty.

Walking past his parents' cottage on the way home from the village today caused a sharp pain deep inside her. He wasn't there and wouldn't be waving from his upstairs window over the garage for another twenty-four months—minus one day.

She looked up, glancing across her own small bedroom. On the desk, a stack of envelopes leaned against her computer. Sulking would get her nowhere. She crossed the powder blue carpet, enjoying its soft thickness against bare feet, and sat, determined to write Ethan at least once a week. She clicked on Word, went into Tools, Letters and Mailings, then into Envelopes. She entered Ethan's mission home address and churned out one hundred and three addressed white envelopes.

* * *

Kim wrote cheerful letters to Ethan right until the day she went into the village to mail his Christmas parcel. She stood in line, waiting for two gray-haired ladies in front to finish chatting with Mrs. Owen who served them, when she sensed someone staring. Turning around, she looked down into the deepest brown eyes she'd seen in three months. His dark curly hair and square chin bore such a resemblance to Ethan that she couldn't hold back a loud gasp. Then she bit her lip, crushed at what she'd done, hoping the young man didn't take her reaction the wrong way.

He smiled at her expression. "It's all right. I'm used to that. My name is Lee Williams." He twisted in his wheelchair, pointing to a middle-aged lady with short brown hair, standing behind him. "And this is my mother. So what's your name?"

"Kim Kendal." She gave an embarrassed laugh. "I'm sorry. I didn't mean to be rude. It's not the wheelchair . . . I was shocked because you look like—"

He interrupted with a quick movement of his hand. "I told you. It's all right." He laughed. "My dad used to say I should offer people my autograph. But being good looking doesn't mean I'm famous, now does it?"

Kim shook her head, grinning, then shrugged her shoulders. "Nothing to stop you working on it though."

Mrs. Williams joined in. "Dear to goodness, that's what I'm always telling him." She pushed strands of straight hair off her forehead. "And if you heard him on the piano, you'd be amazed."

"Was that an invitation, Mam?" Lee asked. He touched Kim's sleeve. "Will you come to our house so I can play for you? You look like a teacher I knew. It's the crooked smile."

Kim hesitated, then gave a soft laugh. "How can I refuse? Besides, I need things to fill my time while my boyfriend's away. Yes, I'll come. As long as you don't live the other side of the valley."

Mrs. Williams scribbled their address while Kim was being served. Kim took the piece of paper from her and hurried to read it. "That's only across the village from me. Won't take me more than ten minutes to get there from home. When can I come?"

Lee looked at his mother and whispered, "Tomorrow?"

Mrs. Williams turned to Kim. "Shall we see you tomorrow, then? At ten?"

Kim nodded and stuffed the paper in her coat pocket, smiling first at Lee and then at all the other people in the queue. When she reached the door, she turned back and waved.

The return journey seemed quick and easy. The swirling fog looked different—softer, more magical. Even passing Ethan's home, tucked away from the road behind tall oak trees, didn't tug at her heart this time. She swung through the creaking field gate behind her parents' cottage. *Ethan told me to meet people, didn't he? And he said, "find treasure."*

She giggled. Was eleven-year-old treasure good enough?

Her stride lengthened. Flinging back her head and taking long breaths of biting air, she let the mounting wind swish at her ponytail, blowing away the past few months of misery along with the fog.

* * *

Christmas came and went before Kim wrote her next letter to Ethan. During that time, she spent more hours at Lee's home than her own. It was New Year's Eve when Mrs. Williams pulled Kim into the kitchen during a visit.

"I have to tell you, dear," she began, and then stopped, her hands twisting and rubbing together, worry lines creasing her forehead. "About our Lee. He never mentions the wheelchair, so neither do I—though I know you must have wondered."

She paused, lips trembling as she glanced at Kim. "But I think you ought to know that despite his young age . . . what I mean . . . what we haven't told you yet, because I never thought you'd get this close, is that he . . ." She finished in a rush. ". . . he has AIDS."

The warmth of the room was overpowering. Kim tried not to show the shock she felt.

Mrs. Williams continued, her words tumbling over each other. "Dear to goodness, now don't go thinking you're in danger." Crossing the room, she reached out to Kim. "You're not at risk. Please don't worry. I'm telling you because . . . because—"

"Please." Kim's tone was gentle. She put her arms around the older woman. "I wasn't thinking of danger. I . . . haven't met anyone with AIDS before. I never realized they were so . . . normal." Kim dropped onto the nearest chair. "What a waste," she whispered, trying to swallow past the tightness in her throat. "What an awful waste. All that talent." She gazed at Mrs. Williams. "He's not just good, you know. On the piano. He's exceptional." Kim put her hands over her face, shaking her head in time with every word. "Why, why, why?"

Mrs. Williams sank onto another chair. "I've asked myself that question so many times." She sighed. "It's the hemophilia, you see. They say he's been harboring AIDS for years. Cross infection, it was. Only recently active." She sat quiet, her shoulders sagging. "But he's never any trouble." Mrs. Williams straightened, leaning toward Kim. "He accepts whatever comes. I dare not think ahead to losing him forever. Making life good for others is his way of getting through it all. Keeps the pain away, he says." She nodded, slowly. "He saw your pain in the Post Office that day, you know. And all the way home he planned for your visit."

A pleading expression came over Mrs. Williams's face. "Shall you still be coming, then? Does it make any difference?"

Kim raised her head as an idea began shaping. She smiled. "Of course I'll come. More than ever. There's so much still to do. You'll be surprised."

She jumped up, flinging her arms once more around an astonished Mrs. Williams. "Have to go now, but I'd like to bring a couple of friends next time—if I may?"

"Why yes, especially if they're anything like as nice as you." She laughed, watching, as Kim whirled into her coat, adding, "Come Thursday, if you can."

Kim nodded. "I'll say goodbye to Lee. Stay in the warm. I can let myself out."

Flinging her crimson scarf over her shoulder, Kim rushed through the hall into the lounge, sending noise and laughter echoing through the house until the front door slammed.

* * *

Late that night Kim sat in her bedroom, writing.

Dear Ethan,

. . .

. . . and so much has happened, you'll never believe. Though knowing you, perhaps you will.

I met an amazing young man. His name is Lee. He's eleven years old and pure treasure. I can now report that in one rainbow slice, the bright parts do outweigh the blues.

The local Elders have agreed to come and listen to Lee's piano music on Thursday, before giving him and his mother the first discussion about The Church of Jesus Christ. Time is really going fast. It's odd how sadness and joy can go together. Please pray with me that Lee will still be alive when you return. You'll love him, too.

Missionary work is a great way to slice rainbows.

Love and handshakes,

Kim

Chapter 16

Mousey or Mighty?

(Sussex Downs, Sussex, England)

If I was honest, I felt like turning into an ostrich, finding a hole for my head, and staying there the rest of my life.

I'd been home three weeks from my mission in Texas, U.S.A.—home being a small village near the Sussex Downs, England—and nothing was going right. My favorite clothes didn't fit—or were no longer in style, friends had moved on, my old car was sold, and the cat had forgotten my smell. The whole world was a crazy place, with wars and calamities and sin in high places every time I turned on the news.

What scared me most was how I seemed to be the only one who cared.

Don't get me wrong. I loved my mission, and my family was the best. But things weren't turning out the way I expected. Members in my home ward said, 'Welcome home, Oliver,' then walked on by as though I'd never been away and not aged a day.

This last one hurt. If they only knew how much older and wiser I'd grown these past two years, I was sure they'd treat me differently. On the other hand, the members hadn't changed a bit. Brother Pickup still smelled of tobacco. Sister Byron wore the same short skirts. Brother Miles still disrupted Gospel Doctrine class with anti-Mormon questions.

On top of all that, my younger brother and sister kept staring at me as though I had handle-with-care stickers pasted all over me.

I tried praying about the problem a couple of times, but nothing changed.

Now the weather had turned. It was the wettest, coldest summer on record, and it was Monday night. I half dozed on the sofa next to Ben and Donna, age sixteen and thirteen, as each family member read in turn from an article in an old New Era dated January, 1994.

I tuned in as Donna read a paragraph, her eyes squinting in the dim light. *"From a returned missionary: Why should I date and get serious with a girl? I'm not sure I even want to marry and bring a family into this kind of world. I'm not sure about my own future . . ."*

Aha! Someone out there knew what it felt like to be me. Ben and Dad read more of the same thing. I grunted, nodding my head.

My turn to read. I was awake now. I agreed with all this. I cleared my throat, ready for more sympathy. *"Well, my, my, my. Isn't that a fine view of things? Sounds like we all ought to go eat a big plate of worms."*

I coughed and slumped in the chair. Before passing the magazine to Dad, I glanced at the previous page to see the author. Oops! President Howard W. Hunter of the Quorum of the Twelve Apostles. One of my heroes. We finished reading, and a phrase stuck in my mind: *Fear is a principal weapon which Satan uses to make mankind unhappy.* I made a mental note to wipe out fear.

Unfortunately, fear made the same kind of note to wipe out me.

It was the following night, and I drove Dad's old black Jag up Thornton Hill, overlooking our valley. The rain had stopped, and everywhere I looked I saw more green trees and fields than in the whole of Texas—or so it seemed. An old friend of mine, Gilly Harper, was with me. She was eighteen, and good for deep talks, so I shared my depression about post mission life as we drove.

At the top of the hill, I turned off the engine and moved sideways to lean against the door. "So. . . that's how I feel."

Gilly raised an eyebrow, mocking me with her slanting blue eyes. "Do you really want to know what I think?"

"You're the only one who won't pull punches. Most people are giving me the hands-off treatment."

"You sound like a rare species." She tossed her short, black hair, sending the curls into a soft halo emphasizing the angular shape of her face.

I smiled. "Around here I am. Maybe endangered." I looked away, frowning. "Seriously. I feel like the whole world is a threat since I came home."

Her left eyebrow shot up. "So England is the whole world?"

"Well . . . yes . . . it's my world. TV brings the rest in."

"Did you expect the world to stop living for two years or something?"

She looked at me like I was a total whacko. I tried to keep a steady voice. "You don't understand. No one does. But I thought at least you would. Apart from the way everyone treats me—like I'm still little Oliver Collins who used to hide in the Primary cupboard—there's this other major scary thing going on with everyone." I thumped the wheel and spoke through clenched teeth. "Apart from three baptisms, what was the point of spending two whole years learning what I've learned, when no one here cares or wants to keep up with me and change their lives for the better?"

Gilly sighed and rolled her eyes. "Cut the drama and calm down."

"But it's important. We're here to progress, right? I've at least learned that much on my mission."

Her gaze softened. "And you did. That's good. But judging the rest of us brings you right down to our level—don't you think?" She gave me a sweet smile that didn't reach her eyes. And up went that eyebrow again.

I wanted to shake her. Instead, I slouched in my seat, silent, not knowing which of my many worries most needed attention. "So I'm wrong, am I? I'm supposed to sit back, take whatever's coming—or not coming—and keep quiet?"

"Nope. Keeping quiet isn't what I meant. What's wrong with

praying for help?"

"I already did. It's like Heavenly Father's forgotten me, now I'm home."

She sighed and tilted her head to one side. "Mousey or Mighty?"

"What?"

"You know—mighty prayer that moves hills like that one behind us." She jabbed her thumb over one shoulder while looking me right in the eye. "Or a mousey it's-never-going-to-work prayer that doesn't make it past your hunky—"

A sudden pounding on the car roof jolted us both upright. Gilly's mouth dropped open. My heart thudded between my ears. A character with a spiked hairdo was moving around the car to my side, still thumping on the roof. He was dressed in shiny black leather. How we missed hearing him arrive on his motorbike, I don't know. He must have turned off the engine and drifted toward us. His sinister face matched his gear as he signalled for me to wind down the window.

Thinking he might smash the glass if I didn't do something, I moved the old fashioned handle half a turn. My voice came out squeaky. "Yes?" I forced the pitch several tones lower and pulled in my jaw. "Yes? What's wrong?"

"You'd better get this heap out of here fast, or you and your babe are in serious trouble. See that over there?" He pointed to the other side of the hill.

I could barely make out a group of motorbikes glinting in the distance.

"And that way?" He waved in the direction of another neighboring valley to the east. More bikes.

I nodded, alarm pulsing behind my eyes.

"Hell's Angels. Rivals." His accent was Cockney, the voice rasping. "There'll be gang warfare in this place in two minutes." He leaned forward, thrusting his whiskered chin toward the crack in the window. "Get it?"

I heard Gilly gasp and knew she was losing it. I put the key in the ignition, fighting to stop the panic. The engine kicked over, and then stalled. One gang roared toward us down the long, winding lane to my right, and our friendly Biker Punk turned full throttle, racing to join them.

I tasted sweat on my upper lip. My fingers wouldn't work. Then Gilly's scream got through to my brain. In a flash, I prayed like I was still a missionary and turned the key again. Nothing. Not even a splutter. Now what? *Please, Father. Help me get Gilly out of here.*

The other gang, tearing up the tarmac from the west, got closer. There was only one path down the hill on our side, and I had to make a hundred and eighty degree turn to reach it— if only we could move. The other two exits were now full of thundering bikes getting nearer by the second. I stole a glance at Gilly. Her face was white and her eyes huge. She was breathing fast. I offered another silent prayer—this time fervent with repentance for losing so much faith.

That's when the miracle began. The engine spun, and life seeped into the old car . . . and into me. We skidded in a circle, tires squealing, and slithered down that hill quicker than ice cream off a red-hot dish. I saw bikes and other black shapes getting smaller and smaller in the rear-view mirror as we left the battlefield behind.

By the time we reached Thornton Village, I could breathe without panting. We didn't talk until I parked outside Gilly's front gate. By then I was laughing, verging on hysterics. I wiped my eyes with the back of one hand. "That's one place I don't want to see again in a hurry."

Gilly gave a shaky smile. "Did you pray, too?"

"Like anything, I did. The hardest since . . . since—"

"Since your mission?"

"Yeah." I gave her a lopsided grin, feeling more than a little foolish at the way I'd been acting. "Yep. The mission habits must have sneaked away for a while. I guess I was expecting too much too soon and worrying about more than I'm supposed to fix. But . . ." I laughed again—this time with more control—and then imitated our sinister friend's gruff voice, "I get it, babe. No more mousey—stick with mighty."

Gilly flashed an impish grin. "Thank goodness for that."

My hand reached for hers. "I should be used to the way prayers are answered, after two years expecting the unexpected. Happens every time. Who'd have thought it would take three people to put me right?"

Gilly looked puzzled. "Three?"

"You, the spiky-haired biker punk, and . . . uh . . . President Hunter."

"Who?"

"He's right. I don't need to eat worms after all."

"Worms?"

She pulled her hand away, and I dropped a kiss on her cheek. "Don't look so worried. There's this excellent article in an old copy of the New Era. You should read it some time. Works today, same as ever. Beats turning into an ostrich."

"Ostrich?"

She opened the door, making a quick exit. I sat for a long time, smiling to myself, giving thanks, and making commitments. My head was out of the sand. Now all I had to do was get a life. I mean, who wants to go around eating worms forever?

Word List

(in case you were wondering)

AMERICAN ENGLISH	BRITISH ENGLISH
Apartment	Flat
Bike seat	Bike saddle
Cabinet	Cupboard
Call you (on phone)	Ring you
Center	Centre
Check book	Cheque book
Dollars	Pounds
Duplex	Semi-detached
Fish & chips restaurant	Chippy
Freeway	Motorway
Front Room	Lounge
Girl	Lass
Idiot	Eeejit (Ireland and Scotland)
Line	Queue
Mailbox	Letterbox
Mom	Mum (England), Mam (Wales)
Movies	Cinema
Movie Star	Film Star
My	Me (England, Ireland)
Myself	Meself
Neighbor	Neighbour
Oh	Och (Scotland)
Paint cans	Paint tins
Pajamas	Pyjamas
Pants	Trousers
Paper route	Paper round
Ride	Lift
Savior	Saviour
Sneakers	Trainers
Very powerful	Right powerful (Yorkshire, Eng)
Yard	Garden
Young lady	Lass
Young man or guy	Lad or boy

About the Author

Anne Bradshaw remembers telling stories before she was nine years old. She discovered that younger siblings stopped fighting if she created wild tales. "It was a fun way to keep them quiet on long car journeys," she says. "I had witches and wizards who slid beneath the tongue, fairies living in people's teeth, and hobgoblins who taunted those poor little fairies until they all but left home, taking bridges, braces, and shiny gold fillings with them."

Anne, who lived in England until she moved to America ten years ago, has written countless articles and short stories for magazines, and has two published books: *Terracotta Summer*, and *Chamomile Winter*.

For many years before moving to America, Anne traveled the British Isles interviewing LDS youth for the *New Era* magazine. "I met some of the finest young people," she says. "Teens are exciting, and it's amazing to be around them."

Anne, and her husband, Bob, have four children and more than a few grandchildren. When not writing, Anne reads any good book she can find, drools over healthy food and fresh fruit (especially warm peaches straight off the tree), and speed walks early mornings.

For more information about Anne, please visit her blog on her website at:

www.annebradshaw.com.